Fleeting City

Library and Archives Canada Cataloguing in Publication

T'ek'gyozyan, Hovhannes, 1974-
[P'akhch'ogh k'aghaksĕ . English]
        Fleeting city / by Hovhannes Tekgyozyan (Jean-Chat Tekgyozyan)
; translated by Neiri Hakhverdi.

Translation of: P'akhch'ogh k'aghaksĕ.
Issued in print and electronic formats.
ISBN 978-1-77161-159-6 (softcover).--ISBN 978-1-77161-160-2 (HTML).--
ISBN 978-1-77161-161-9 (PDF)

I. Hakhverdi, Nairi, translator II. Title. III. Title: P'akhch'ogh
k'aghaksĕ. English.

PK8549.T45P3513 2017   891'.99236   C2017-902200-8
                                                      C2017-902201-6

Published by Mosaic Press, Oakville, Ontario, Canada, 2017.

MOSAIC PRESS, Publishers

Copyright © 2017 Արամ Պաչյան, Aram Pachyan

Published in Agreement with ARI Literary and Talent Agency

Translated by Nairi Hakhverdi

Cover Design by Eric Normann / Interior Design by Courtney Blok

We acknowledge the Ontario Arts Council
for their support of our publishing program
We acknowledge the Ontario Media Development Corporation
for their support of our publishing program

Funded by the   Financé par le
Government   gouvernement   Canada
of Canada   du Canada

MOSAIC PRESS
1252 Speers Road, Units 1 & 2
Oakville, Ontario L6L 5N9
phone: (905) 825-2130

info@mosaic-press.com

Fleeting City

BY HOVHANNES TEKGYOZYAN
(Jean-Chat Tekgyozyan)

Translated by Nairi Hakhverdi

Translator's Note

It goes without saying that translation, or the process of translating, invariably poses challenges and dilemmas for the translator. In the case of of Hovhannes Tekgyozyan's novel, my challenge began at the very top: with the very title itself, Fleeting City.

Luckily, city was not problematic. There is only one word in Armenian for "city"-- քաղաք (qaghaq)--which smoothly translates into "city" in English. My choice for fleeting, on the other hand, was justifiably disputable.

For fleeting, there were four problems I needed to resolve: ambiguity, discourse, frequency, and inflection.

Ambiguity: the Armenian verb փախչել (p'axchel) can mean both to run away and to vanish rapidly. Tekgyozyan playfully uses both meanings interchangeably.

Discourse: փախչել (p'axchel) is a common verb in Armenian, used formally, informally, and colloquially.

Frequency: the verb is sprinkled throughout the text, not only in the title.

Inflection: the verb in Armenian is regular and is inflected in the present, past, simple, continuous, perfect, and gerund.

My most common-sense solution was: find one verb that solves all four problems and stick with it throughout the text. Another solution could have been to use a set of verbs to mix and match depending on the sentence or context. For instance, I could have translated: "Our building probably jumped one street to the right" in one sentence and "Amiryan Street escaped unexpectedly" in another. However, since Tekgyozyan repeats the title verb thematically in his novel, this latter solution would have carried its own problems.

After many hours of testing and trying out different options, I finally settled on to fleet, but not without reservations. Fleet resolves all but one problem: it is not generally used informally or colloquially in English. However, since the novel is literary in nature, I argued with myself that on this occasion, in this context, it should be acceptable to draw a discursive difference between the source text in Armenian and the target text in English without comprising the general style of the rest of the novel

Nairi Hakhverdi

Fleeting City

I live in a *fleeting* city.

The word *fleeting* seemed strange just now. Am I wrong? How can letters come together like that and make my city fleet? I repeated the word a few times, scribbled it on a piece of paper, and understood that to describe Yerevan, the word *fleet* also *fleets*.

Winter is not like summer. In my city, the difference between summer and winter is so great that it seems as if I'm living two lives, as if I'm two people who never meet. In the winter, my house is in some indefinite place outside of the city. In the summer, I live in the city center, right on Abovian Street. And when I come out of my apartment in the center, it feels like I'm still inside.

With my eyes still closed, I recalled the summer. I absorbed on my mother's scent through my sweat, jumped up, and drew back the curtain. My mother had sewn a curtain from a dark fabric to keep out the summer. The sun was stinging.

I knew that I was late--it must be around twelve. The second sign of my being late rang one minute later. I always forget to turn off the buzzing of my phone. Grigor's impatience was burning among the red numbers.

"Gagik, are you home?"

"I was sleeping," the word sleeping did not fit Yerevan in July. "Where are you?"

"Under the Square clock. [1] Hurry up! When will you be here?"

"In half an hour..."

"Half an hour!" The city poured into my phone, the smell of lahmajoon struck my nose and compelled me to brush my teeth. I spat out the white and took off my underwear. Did the pictures turn to the wall in shame? Hard to imagine... Our building probably *fleeted* one street to the right.

Water was pouring down on me like needles. My mother's scent was everywhere in the room. I'm going to draw. I've arranged everything frame by frame. All I need to do now is create movement. The movement of scent. It is the only thing that comprises my biography in this *fleeting* city.

The sound of the car horn reached my house all the way to Sayat-Nova Avenue. I was about to include that... that bastard's head in my cartoon. I was under the Square clock in five minutes.

"Hey," Grigor--Grig--is swallowed up into my car so fast that it leaves me dumbfounded. He's not swallowed up; he's suddenly transplanted into my car. "This is the first time I'm seeing you in a suit, in this heat at that."

"Sit... It would've been good if you'd also worn a suit."

"Why? Where are we going?"

"Heaven... There will be hundreds of officials."

"Your dad, too?"

---

1 Square refers to Republic Square, the central square in the city center of Yerevan. The clock refers to the clock on the façade of the Ministry of Finance on Republic Square.

"Probably."

"Listen, did you draw your cartoon?"

"No."

"They'll kick you out of college."

"They won't kick me out..."

"You're making an animation about scent. You couldn't come up with a lighter theme?"

"Like what?"

"Like Little Red Riding Hood and the lumberjack..."

Amiryan Street appeared unexpectedly. My car turned around and somehow found itself in front of the pharmacy on Zakyan.

Ever since I was a kid, I've thought of pharmacies as swimming pools with people swimming inside of them. The smell reminded me of the mumps I got when I was five, which is why I projected the features of a pig [2] on the roly-poly woman cleaning the windows.

"What do you want to buy?" Grig's gaze was still on Amiryan Street.

"Scissors, to cut your hair with."

"Hm, look at your own hair. They've messed it up so bad, you look like an Apache."

"Is there anything you'd like?" The saleswoman was smiling broadly behind the window with thick smudged makeup on her face.

"It's my birthday today. I'm turning twenty-one."

"Congratulations." As a gift, the saleswoman's gown opened up a little. Something rustled inside, chilling the back of my neck. "You didn't say what you wanted."

"What should we take?"

Grig had not yet recovered from the heat of the Square.

---

2 In Armenian, the mumps are called "khozuk," which also means "piglet." The connection between pigs and the mumps becomes more apparent as the story progresses.

"Vitamins," he said and laughed loudly.

"Here you go. Please pay at the counter."

"And ten condoms. The best ones."

Grigor's mouth stayed fixed on the orange of the vitamin-advertising poster, wide open and painted like Munch's The Scream: unaddressed, startled, and horrified at who knows what or at everything.

"Here you go. Please pay at the counter."

The starchy flaps of the saleswoman's gown suddenly and simultaneously opened up, revealing a gigantic tail between her firm, clean-shaven thighs that reached all the way down to her ankles. The scales breathed and moved in a peculiar way. The beginning of the tail was in the woman's vagina. The scissor-like limb covered her feet.

"You know what I want?"

"Give me one..."

"Would you like someone to talk to you through an interview?"

"What interview? I'm not going abroad, am I?"

"They would talk to you, but talk to you as if they were interviewing you..."

"I don't know. You lied, didn't you? Your birthday is in November."

The pharmacy stayed behind the turn, drowned in water.

Lili's feline snout appeared by itself on billboards, in cell phones, and on the walls of newly started buildings. She was a real cartoon heroine: a princess, a non-existent character that you try to make real. And then you move around the limbs, rearrange the body, and stick the wings of an angel on her without forgetting to first tie one of her legs to a table. You close your eyes as she flies into wash-ing powder, slides over the brim of an ice-cream, and... gives you a wet dream.

Grig was the one who introduced us.

Lili dreamed of becoming an actress, so Grig intro-duced her to a young stage director who was allegedly a relative of mine. The director didn't say anything con-crete, but he suggested she be present during rehearsals.

On the third day of watching rehearsals, the doors of the theater opened, and the witch mother of the prin-cess, sitting on a broomstick, began to circle around me. I never saw the mother's face in its entirety--she always appeared in parts, from a magnified perspective, as if she had been zoomed in. The piecemeal, magnified appear-ance of the witch mother's face helped me not to have to look into her eyes.

But one time I got really scared. It was after our first night, or, more correctly, our first evening--Lili had to be home by ten--that the witch appeared in her entirety, without a broomstick, and even with a little makeup.

Lili had barely managed to get into the car when the city unexpectedly skidded. I braked. Baghramyan Avenue was in a strange position: the beginning and end were not visible.

There was a rally by the president's residence. Those gathered held up banners discolored from the heat, de-manding either an explanation for the death or the death penalty. Like a stealthy thief on his toes, my car was work-ing on circumventing the ralliers when an old woman with disheveled wiry hair threw a bottle of Noy[3] at us and yelled:

----

3 Noy is a brand of bottled water in Armenia.

"Damn you, aren't you supposed to be the youth of this nation?"

A few Ivan-the-Terrible-looking police officers pulled out their clubs, but Baghramyan--the avenue, not the Marshal-- [4] brought us two streets away.

"That was easy," Grig unfastened his tail. "It's hot... Can we stop and have coffee somewhere before getting to heaven?"

Lili was quiet.

"Let's stop..."

I don't like coffee houses buried in red, but what could I do? I braked. Grig--I don't know--he probably went to the bathroom. Lili sat across from me, opened up her bag, took out an ancient dictaphone, and turned it on:

"Gagik, talk a little about your family. How is your relationship with your parents?"

"I love my parents very much, but we are completely different people. I remember one time, in fifth grade, we were learning about 'Ancient India' in our 'Ancient World History' class. I studied and gave the book to my mother to check if I'd studied correctly. My mother listened and said it was fine. I went to school and got a two. [5] From that day on, I figured that I could only ever rely on myself."

"How was your relationship with your father when you were a child? Did you play often? Did you talk?"

"No, we didn't play. We probably played very little. But I remember that in the evenings, around nine o'clock, I would pretend to fall asleep so that he would come and take me to bed."

....
4 Baghramyan Avenue is named after Marshal Baghramyan, a Soviet Armenian military commander during World War II

5 In the Soviet grading system, a two out of five is more or less equivalent to a U.S. grade D.

"And did you have any desire to be like him when you were growing up?"

"No."

"Did you have any inferiority complexes when you were young?"

"I have one now! When I was young I was sure I would become an influential man."

"What year of your life do you consider to be a turning point?"

"When I was five... And probably the year that has not ended yet."

"Do you remember your grandfathers?"

"One of them died two months after I was born; the other much earlier."

"And your grandmothers?"

My lips moved towards Lili's lips. Grig appeared between our mouths.

"Are you done with your interview?" he gulped his coffee down in one go. "Let's go?"

The bodyguards had planted themselves around the swimming pool with dark sunglasses around their eyes and headsets in their noses and ears. A few officials, pale as lords, were playing golf.

We each took a glass of wine. Lili's feline snout began to photograph itself with the intention of appearing on the cover of some elite magazine.

"Don't forget to give me one," Grig had not forgotten about the condoms. "I saw a nice chick."

The seconds slowed down. In slow-motion I drew my hand into my pocket, took out the condom, and... The seconds flew by in fast-forward. My father's hand and his gray-specked beard, which resembled the melting peak of Ararat, [6] appeared somewhere between the wine glass and the condom.

"What are you drinking?" He picked up the glass and took a sip. "How are you?"

The condom froze in the air for two, three seconds and then appeared in Grigor's palm.

"Good..."

"Is your mother here?"

"She left two days ago."

"I see. You never come around. Your sister is asking about you all the time. Call at least."

"I'll call..."

"Take good care of your mother," he said, shoving his index finger and middle finger in my belt. "You've lost weight... The President liked the swimming pool a lot, but he can't stay more than half an hour. He has a meeting. You'll take good care of yourself, right? Don't drink too much..."

He left, wiping his dripping beard.

I was five when my parents divorced. My father was seeing a woman who was expecting a child. A month after the divorce, she had a girl.

Both the girl and the woman are very good to me. I love my sister very much. When we were kids, we would meet every other day and play. Because of her job, my mother was often absent from the city, so she left me in the charge of my grandmother.

I remember the day she was preparing to leave for two months. I held her for one hour, not letting her walk, move, or talk. She left. My only consolation was her scent,

---

6 Mount Ararat, now located in eastern Turkey, can be observed from many parts of western Armenia, including Yerevan.

which seemed to have stayed behind in me. For more than a week I couldn't smell anything else.

It was a Sunday. My father came and took me to their house. My sister skipped around in joy, ran up to me, hugged me, and stroked my mother's scent. Her crime made me cry in pain, so I took her to the balcony and beat her with a broom. My father came out and slapped me. Until then he had never touched me. His fingers were imprinted on my chin like the tricolor of the Armenian flag...

The President left an hour later.

At around four, those who had gathered downed their drinks and filled the pool. The swimsuits of both the sunbathing men and women skipped from one body to another like butterflies. At six o'clock, the jazz that was born out of coffee cups gathered us around the table.

"I'd like you to meet. This is Edita," Grig appeared next to me arm-in-arm with an octopus woman whose looks did not correspond to an "Edita." "She knows English. She came with the committee..."

Lili frowned her feline snout and instantly understood that she does not understand English.

"Can you believe it?" For a moment I saw Grig in an eight-legged cage. "She says there's a place in Armenia called 'Heaven's Door.' She's come to see it and I said I know the place. Huh, why aren't you saying anything?"

"He's sad. Do you have glue on you?"

"Your shoe fell apart?"

Vahagn's arrival raised a wave of happiness. Even I, who don't like him, got happy. Vahagn has only two moods: with weed and without weed. He gloated with the smile of a wolf. That meant that you could put whatever he had brought under Baku [7] and get the entire city high.

Four months ago, at a similar gathering, Vahagn's mood was so good that the club almost turned into an airport. But Grig and I managed to get away. Who knows who had announced our weed program to one of the private TV stations. Thank God Grig's now ex-girlfriend worked at that station. For one hour we were locked up in the women's bathroom waiting for that dreadful Judgment Day to end. If the son of one of the officials had not appealed to weapons for help, we would have been able to speak the same language with the journalists.

The next day, the Prime Minister appealed to the government urging temperance and moderation from the members and their families. For one week, my father was walking around gloating: "You saw, didn't you? You saw that my son is not involved in those things! He's a decent, intelligent man--an artist."

Lili wanted to leave.

"Mom called. She wasn't feeling well. I don't want you to come. I want to be alone; I want to think a little. I'm seeing my father in two days. He doesn't know I'm a big girl. More correctly... He hasn't seen me in five years. Bye..."

Grigor had no intention of staying either.

"I'll take the chick to the hotel and then we'll see. You'll call, no?"

I called a cab. On the other side of the street a benefactress had built herself a Versailles. The Greek gods and *tripterous* angels did not help ward off evil. The witch mother's magnified nose pushed itself between my and Lili's lips, and the cab ran after the *fleeting* city to the Fif-

7 Baku is the capital city of Azerbaijan.

teenth Quarter. [8]

The pool was filled with needles.

For a moment I remembered the photographs on the wall and Lili's snout appeared on my phone.

"Almost home."

Vahagn had started working on rolling a joint. The smokes emptied fast, filled up, burned, got slobbered, were passed from mouth to mouth.

Text message... Text message... Text message...

The limbs of the smoke spread inside of me. A little more and a fish tail would have grown out of my penis.

Grig was flapping around in the octopus' cage. My laughter made the bras and panties hanging from the clothesline fly up, circle around, and embrace each other in the air.

"How's your mother? My kitten."

I didn't get around to mentioning the witch mother's name. She latched onto my brain like a tick and sucked out my happiness. Thank God I only saw her face for a moment, after which a close-up photograph of her nose was taken as she flew up with her nostrils flared, sniffing the panties.

Text message... Text message... Text message...

With a choking whirr in my throat I saw how the faces of those present were getting erased. Only the Munchian mouths remained, open and painted on the orange of the sun. The joint, which was going into one mouth and coming out of another, had our lips lined up on the thread of its smoke. My mother's scent was not coming out of me.

I drowned.

The blades of the water depicted the old woman's Bib-

8 A residential district in Yerevan.

lical face. For a moment the scribbled mouth remained open and frozen on the tricolor of the Armenian flag:

"Damn you, aren't you supposed to be the youth of this nation?"

My city *fleeted* again. We are hiking to the center with Nork's First Quarter [9] and the monument of Gai [10] held up. The walls of the buildings are suddenly plastered with an assortment of political campaigns, pictures of candidates, and the heads of bulls.

Vahagn's wolf smile was circling around kissing the walls. Finally it stopped in my ear and whispered:

"Did you notice? Her nipples look like zits."

I wasn't sure who he was talking about, but the fish tail made itself felt.

My laughter dried up. The orange of the sun, with traces of Munchian lipstick on it, was in a glass. I drank it.

I wasn't feeling well in the pimply pool. The air in my lungs was swimming from one end to another. I went back and forth once or twice without paying attention to the flapping of my tail.

A mouth with a cigarette hanging from it approached me.

"You don't have enough breath," it said. "You can't drown."

I don't know why, but I kissed it, cigarette and all.

The keypad on my phone worked. The numbers of the phone numbers were changing by the second, growing bigger and smaller. My father's phone number was turning into my mother's. The numbers were changing around so

---

9 Nork is a residential district in Yerevan.
10 Commander Gai (Haik Bzhshkyants) was crowned a hero for his role in the Russian Civil War of 1918-1921. There is a statue commemorating him in Nork.

fast that I couldn't see whose number was whose.

"Did you screw that octopus?"

"I love you, love you, want you..."

Catching its breath for a second, my phone anxiously signaled that I had new messages.

"Gag... What octopus? If you're going to write words like that, don't write at all. Lili"

"Gagik, have you lost your mind? You love me and want me? Go home and sleep. Grig"

The faces were suddenly restored. I had just come out of the swimming pool when Vahagn was rubbing his pimply chest--no, face--on the walls and shouting:

"L... Let's go... That Gai... Gai... Gay... Wherever he is, he'll show up soon..."

So after a successful hike from Nork's First Quarter to the center, it comes here. My suit dressed me by itself and hurled me into my car. My city *fleeted*, flying me through clouds and washing powder.

There were red specks on the morning.

My grandmother is feeling proud, saying that her village is the first in Armenia where raspberries ripen. At dawn: red specks. I flew and picked the red raspberries from the white.

My grandmother was sitting on the threshold with her five-meter-long hair tied up. She saw me and embraced my head with her limbed hair.

"Is your mother roaming abroad again?"

I drove the pigs away from the gate and went inside.

The stairs, worn more and more each day, bared the wizened legs of the house. It was like those walking huts in Russian fairy tales. But in all the years that I've come and gone, I've never seen my grandmother's house *fleet*.

"Grandma, stop moving around! Come, sit down, tell me how you are."

My grandmother's hair wrapped itself around the stones, the grapevines, the gate's handle, swept the floor and stroked the foundations, and then pressed against me and loved me.

"I'm fine. Your father isn't coming?"

"I saw him yesterday... He didn't say anything. You come... Your daughters-in-law love you very much and so do your grandchildren."

"Take good care of that child." The hair tossed two, three pieces of wood in the wood stove and kindled the fire. "What do you want me to make for you?"

"Which child?"

"Your sister..."

"Grandma, don't you think it's time you stopped relying on this wood stove? Isn't it sad that you have to cut this much wood summer and winter just to cook one meal?"

"Instead of talking so much, get your hair cut. You're not a girl."

"Don't tell me you heard something stupid from one of your neighbors."

"No, no, my child, what neighbors? And then, I'm not one to listen to those idiots."

"Have the swallows come again?"

My grandmother leaves the windows open in the spring so that swallows can come and weave a nest in her house.

"They came and laid a few chicks."

"Where are they?"

"In your uncle's room."

My phone chirped and for the first time I saw that

my grandmother's hair was very similar to the feet of the house. There was only one difference: the feet didn't walk.

"Bless you, science, what is this?"

"I bought a new phone."

"I've seen phones, but this thin?"

The hair took the phone, played with the buttons, and turned on the voice recorder.

"Grandma, do you remember when and where you were born?"

"I was born in 1927 in our village. It's the most important date of my life. I've lost all the other dates just like I've lost my children. If you changed the dates around, nothing would change."

"Did you have any friends until you went to school?"

"I finished four grades. My last friend died two years ago. I have a notebook. There's something about everyone in it."

"Will you show me the notebook at the end of this?"

"The pages of my notebook are like swallows: they come off, fly away, and then come back and gather again."

"And of those who left, are there many of them?"

"I write so I don't forget. There are many who are still alive."

"Do you see noticeable changes in your family structure since you were born?"

"Many. My father and mother passed away, then my daughter was stillborn, then the twins were poisoned and died when they were three. My son didn't see thirty springs, my grandson has his name, and the elder became the victim of a bullet. The last one to go was my old man. But, thank God, boy, I have two grandchildren. There is a Jesus on the mountain."

"When you say 'There is a Jesus on the mountain,' what do you mean?"

"That mountain church of ours is one of the oldest."

"And, grandma, did you marry in love?"

"I don't know how it happened. One day I was coming home from the mountain, they called me and said, 'Your village boy wants you.'"

"And why is your hair so long?"

When my mother was pregnant with me, she vowed that if I were a boy, she would name me after her father. She hadn't turned six yet when my stonemason grandfather got stuck under the ruins of a bridge and died. But two months before I was born I already had a name. My uncle, not thirty yet, died, leaving me his name and the terror of carrying the memory of a dead person.

I was only a child, but I could clearly see the pain of my grandmother who had lost four children and the guilt of my mother who was orphaned. Each time my mother returns from abroad, she says that I take more and more after my father as time passes.

We had come to the village to celebrate New Year's Eve.

On December 30, red specks dropped from a neighboring Azerbaijani village. It was the sound of thunder, but no rain fell. And then someone shouted:

"Run! They're missiles!"

I was pulling the tail of a pig, wanting it to flee, too. My grandmother's four-meter-long hair swept aside snow, clutched at tree branches, and went into houses through their windows looking for me. It found me and picked me up.

I was five, but I understood from the red specks that

my uncle had died. A mine had blown up in front of the house. My grandmother's hair grew one meter in front of my eyes.

"Get into the bomb shelter," shouted the neighbor who had built a shelter in the basement of his house.

We were at the base of the house when they saw that I was infected with the mumps. Naturally I didn't say that I had gotten infected from pulling the tail of a pig. They tried to get me to the city somehow. My father couldn't come--he was in the trenches. I remember my mother's wails and cries--it was that day that she found out about her husband's affair and the child that had been born from that affair.

A Beetle was taking us to Yerevan. I was so scared I couldn't breathe. My grandmother had often told me about the king who had turned into a pig. And it was right then, at that moment that I understood that the city was *fleeting*. You come closer and she flies away and leaves. And however much you beg, telling her you're sick, it's all the same, she won't listen, she'll *fleet* again.

A few years later, my father was awarded an official position for defending the borders of the homeland and for being the brother of a hero. The current president had been to those places and knew my father.

There were red specks on the following morning, too.

"When is your mother going again?" the hair couldn't get enough of me.

"I don't know, but I'll come back soon... And tell your son to lay a water pipe to the house. It's sad that you have to fetch so much water every day from the spring."

"It doesn't bother me. Take good care of that child..."

"Grandma, are you saying I should get my hair cut?"

"It's up to you, son... If only I had gathered some raspberries for you to take with you..."

My car flew, leaving behind my grandmother's hopes on her unmoving house and the church on the mountain.

The village road is like a turtle. My car is driving in fast-forward until the church door; that is, if you want to call it a church. They say that it's a fourth-century construction. It's not even two meters in diameter and I'll refrain from mentioning the missing cupola. The Turks are trying to prove that the monastery was an old Azerbaijani mosque, not taking into account that there are cross-windows in the walls and the reliefs of heads of domesticated animals under the cupola. I was very scared of those carvings as a child. When it got foggy, they would detach from the church, fly up, and stick to the sky like imprints. The heads of star-swallowing bulls.

In slow-motion I put my hand into my pocket. My fingers collided with the sticky condom. What made me buy ten of them? I recalled the octopus. I don't know whether it was the presence of the condom or the sexual relation that had taken place between the octopus and Grig, but the fish tail made itself felt. The seconds flew by in fast-forward, filling the frame with images of dying villages, people, and a *quavering* lake. My city was not waiting for me. And that's why it didn't manage to *fleet*.

With my eyes still closed, I thought about the summer. The black wanted to remind me of something. I jumped up and drew the curtain. The smell of *lahmajoon* stung. I lit a cigarette. My insides had dried up like smoked fish. It's good that I hadn't forgotten to turn off the buzz of my phone. Lili had called. I called back. Once, twice, five times. She was out of reach. Could it be that the thread that had tied my angel's leg to the table had been cut?

"Grig, hi..."

"Where are you?" Grigor's "hello" had dried up in the sun.

"At home..."

"We've been calling you every five minutes."

"What happened?"

"Nothing. Your girlfriend flew to Rome half an hour ago, to her father."

I took on my mother's scent through my sweat and sweated some more.

"I forgot... I'm coming now."

"Where are you coming?"

Davit's statue [11] grew between me and Lili. The witch mother was flying and sweeping the dust off Davit's penis with her broom.

"But you're really bad, you know?"

"Lil, forgive me, please, i was sleeping, promise that you won't love an italian."

"So, what happened?"

"Nothing. I'm writing a text."

"Have you completely lost your mind? It'll die before it reaches the air."

"What'll die?"

"Your text. You've never received dead texts?"

"No, and I don't even know what that is."

"A text message that you wrote but that the addressee only receives much later."

"What are you babbling about?" In my head Davit

---

11 Davit of Sasun is a legendary Armenian hero who fought off Arab invaders in the early Middle Ages. A statue of him at the entrance of Yerevan train station depicts him on a rearing horse.

wanted to urinate.

"Gagik, Edita called yesterday."

"What Edita? Oh, the octopus?"

"No, the fish tail. In short, she's asking to be taken to 'Heaven's Door.'"

"You know where it is?"

"Vahagn will know. Isn't it around Sevan? Can you be near the Opera [12] in half an hour?"

I turned off my phone with the dead text message. Lili's feline snout stuck like an imprint on the sky. And the witch flew up with her broomstick and sat on the tail of the airplane.

Until he was sixteen, Vahagn looked like his kindergarten picture. He was given the role of little Santa Claus in his New Year's play. After the play, the real Santa Claus had complimented Vahagn and given him a white rubber parrot. Then he had squeezed the gift so that the boy could learn the only way to make the bird sing. While the little Santa Claus was inhaling the air that was coming out from under the squeezed parrot, the big Santa Claus disappeared. Taken by surprise, the toy tried to fly away. Naturally its efforts were in vain, since the toy makers had not detached the bird's wings from its body. Being child lovers of the highest order, they could not allow the bird to escape from a child's hands. Vahagn had crouched down to pick up the toy and had seen, through the crack of the door, how the real Santa Claus was taking off his ancient robe and kissing the senior teacher, Miss Knarik.

"This one was crap."

I understood from Vahagn's canine look that you

---

12 The Opera is short for the Opera House. It is located in central Yerevan.

couldn't even lift the dying houses of Kond [13] with what he had brought.

"Vahagn," Grig was slobbering on the smoke with one eye on the map, "do you know a place called 'Heaven's Door'? There's someone from abroad I need to take there."

"Man or woman? Is he or she nice at least?"

"Not very, to be honest..."

"Grig, I've known you for a thousand years. You wouldn't take anyone to heaven without getting something in return. Be careful, those foreigners have a million diseases."

Grig's fingers went into my pocket in slow-motion, scratched my thigh in fast-forward, took out the condoms, and twirled them in the air like rings. One of them went to Vahagn.

"You're a real clown, you know? Bring her here. There's no better heaven than this."

"No, seriously, you don't know?"

There was a time when Grig and Vahagn were close friends, even though they lived a hundred kilometers apart. Grig listened to and quoted System of a Down, [14] whereas Vahagn barely knew who Stevie Wonder was.

Sometimes when it got late--Vahagn didn't live in the city at the time--they would go to Grigor's house.

In the mornings, to eliminate the smell in the bathroom, Grig would throw a lit cigarette in the sink, for which he got scolded by his mother for having bad manners and not taking care of his health.

Grigor had only stayed one day at Vahagn's house;

13 One of the oldest residential districts in Yerevan.
14 System of a Down is an Armenian-American rock band.

more precisely, one night and one tragicomic morning. At around six o'clock, Grig had gotten out of the inflatable village bed to relieve himself of his natural needs. He had opened the bathroom door and... Vahagn's mother had been in there.

In the morning, without eating breakfast and with all his needs left intact, Grig said, "My mother isn't feeling well. They've taken her to the hospital," and fled to the city.

"'Heaven's Door'... I'll look now. I know for sure there's a 'Crow's Gate.'

"Isn't that in Turkey or, more precisely, in Western Armenia?" [15]

"Why are your nipples sticking out?" Vahagn's face became "childlike" for a moment, resembling his kindergarten picture.

"My nipples are always erect." What else was I supposed to say to that pimply idiot?

"You're pregnant, that's why." System of a Down's pain kept Grig's mouth open and drawn on the map of Armenia like a modern version of "The Motherland Calls." [16]

"Asshole..."

I wanted to punch him for those inane words, but, soothed by my Homeland's , I bit his shoulder in a brotherly way instead. What modern? What System? Grig's mouth, frozen from the pain of being open, produced a quote from the woven melody about the massacres at the beginning of the last century.

"Hey, isn't there a 'Parrot's Gate'?" Vahagn's hopes to

15 Western Armenia refers to the historically Armenian territories that were lost at the hands of the Turks during the genocide of 1915.

16 "The Motherland Calls" is a statue commemorating the Battle of Stalingrad in World War II. It is situated in Volgograd, Russia.

"fly" failed and his laugh didn't catch on.

"Isn't it around Sevan?"

Last year we went to Sevan for a day.

"Slow down!" Grig was scared of two things: speed and dogs. To overcome the second fear, his psychologist had advised him to get a dog. The little defenseless beast, after being left hungry for two days, attacked Grig and bit his leg, a crime for which the dog was immediately replaced by a Persian cat.

Whatever you could think of was sold on the way: from stone-baked bread to ancient bathing suits. But it soon became clear that the most lucrative business was the floral business. Every three to four kilometers along the edge of the highway, there were wreaths fastened to red signposts pointing to flower shops nearby.

We swam and sizzled, and with purple sunstrokes on our skulls, we returned home. On the way, Grig remembered his TV star girlfriend who didn't carry the prefix "ex-" yet, and decided to buy her wild flowers.

The shop by the first wreath was closed. Around the second wreath there wasn't even a trace of such an "establishment." A few kilometers down, when we approached the third wreath, we saw a mound of soil with a sad cross on it and a fountain with fresh flowers next to it.

"There is a 'Heaven's Door'... It's around Sevan's church."

Vahagn was sixteen when he met two men smoking in a peculiar way on his way home. He asked for a cigarette. One of the smokers lingered, but when he discovered that he was only sixteen and didn't have "the manners of a man," he offered him a joint.

"Don't tell anyone."

Vahagn at first didn't understand what it was he shouldn't tell--that he didn't have the manners of a man or that smoking harms your health? And, with that same uncertainty, it's already been six years that Vahagn has been carrying out his weed program. Don't tell anyone...

One thing was clear to Vahagn: after that incident he no longer looked like his kindergarten picture.

"Let's go..."

Grig wrapped Armenia's "female" face and got up. Vahagn remained seated. The circling stars above his head brought up feelings of New Year's Eve.

After his father died, Grig lived with his mother. A few years ago, his sister, in the hopes of finding a comfortable life, was given asylum in one of the European countries.

Five minutes after we enter, Grigor's house, garden, furniture, and household utensils start to melt and crystallize. All that remains in the end are the missed smile of his mother on the white of the glass, the paws of the priest cat stretched toward the disk of the sun, and the writing on the wall, "*Ne dazhdyoshsya menya, petlya.*" [17]

Grig was packing his stuff in fast-forward. Underwear entered and tangled up in shirtsleeves; T-shirts swelled up and choked in the mouths of jeans.

The seconds slowed down when the chain of the bag was pulled. Grig's right hand extended in fast-forward to grab the handle while his left stroked the cat that was playing with the sun. For a moment his mother's smile only appeared on the white, after which the seconds flew by in fast-forward, stealing us through the narrow throat of the gate. The city ran. Grig's mother's words were tied

17 Russian for "You won't get to me, noose."

to the back of my car like ribbons:

"Where are you going on an empty stomach?"

My city was *fleeting* through the mouth of the gorge. I stopped right before reaching Tsitsernakaberd:[18]

"What happened?"

"I want to call Lili..."

"And you think this is the right time to do so? We still have to get to the store, buy food..."

"I'll be right back..."

"Where are you going?" The "packed" clothes popped out of the bag choking Grig, "To the hairdresser's?"

I wanted to be bald. The noise and wind of the city were in my hair. Every day I combed the information and smeared gel on it. My hair... It's like an antenna. And all I want is to rest, to not think about the trees that are cut, the war that's not ending and was never started, or the idiots kneeling at my city's throat. To be honest, I'm afraid of the pain in my head repeating.

Three years ago a beast with crooked legs and a crooked neck called me a "son of a bitch." He caught my fist in the air, pulled out my hair, and shoved a newspaper in my face. It was my father's picture. They accused my father--not his picture--of corruption.

I didn't say anything to my father. The noise, the wind, the letters in the newspaper filled in my hair and boiled like lead. When we were kids we played a strange game. We would carve out a cross in tuff, boil lead, and pour it into the carving. I couldn't take it anymore. I went home and shaved off my burning hair. But I wasn't able to carve out a cross.

"Should I cut it?" The hairdresser in a white gown was

---

18 Armenian Genocide memorial.

preparing the surgical instruments.

"Cut it with scissors."

When the evil scissors touched the back of my neck, I remembered the sparrows that had built a nest in my grandmother's house. The wings of my hair flapped one last time and became waste--they are no longer a part of me.

"Shave the rest."

Grig held his stomach when he saw my bald head.

"But it's not bad... Anyway, my cat will like you."

"Do I look like a priest?"

Grig's jaw dropped and froze when he heard his voice on the radio.

"Grigor, has there ever been someone for you that you considered an authority and wanted to resemble?"

"John Lennon. A man whom I could consider my teacher."

"Were you loved in your family as a child? Were you the center of attention for the adults?"

"Yes, my mother always said that my ancestors owned great estates in Western Armenia. Many of them were killed during the Genocide. Should justice be served and we get our share of lands back, it's very possible that I will be proclaimed the prince of Cilicia." [19]

"Have there ever been moments when your imagination tried to swallow you and muffle your reason?"

"Never. Imagination is a whole born out of reality's shreds. For example, of my childhood love, only one image has survived. On Pushkin Street, in the corner across

19 The Armenian Kingdom of Cilicia, now located in south-east Turkey, was established in the 12th century and fell in the 14th century. Armenians continued to live there until the genocide of 1915.

from Pioneer Cinema, there was a house that they have now torn down. The color of the bricks of that house and the smile of the girl looking out of the window have survived in my memory. I don't remember her face, but her smile is in front of my eyes. It's as if I made all of this up."

"Do you consider yourself a lucky person?"

"There was a time when I thought a lot about that. Lucky in what sense? Either way, if I had an opportunity to change my destiny, I probably wouldn't take it."

"Have you ever had suicidal thoughts?"

"Never. I see suicide as being an escape from one reality to another where it's almost the same reality as here. One of my friends says he lives in a *fleeting* city."

"So it seems that cities can also commit suicide. Grigor, there is a strange text in your room. Did you write it?"

"Everyone writes about their room in their own words."

"And what does it say?"

"*Ne dazhdyoshsya menya, petlya...*"

Lili was out of reach. Her mother probably forced her to visit Davit. And that beast is naked summer and winter. He could at least wear underwear.

There was a red ring around my text message, which meant that it was stuck in the air, that it had not reached anywhere. The ring gave me hope: apparently my message hadn't died yet.

"Edi-ta," Grig was like a drug addict. He breathed the octopus' name greedily and endlessly.

Yerevan spun us like a roulette and hurled us to the right. The images born out of the speed lined up side by side and were enumerated.

The process had merged one image into another. Two

of the streets had succumbed to an accident while spitting in each other's mouths. And the Opera building, stuck in their intersection, was trying to readjust its wretched position.

I remembered my virtual past when I saw Edita.

The year before last I spent six to eight hours roaming the Internet. It was winter.

I already mentioned on one occasion that my house is in an indefinite place in the winter, and that place is probably the Internet.

The unexpected flights of my city forced me to find unknown faces, even though those faces were often without features.

The greatest invention after the "Theory of Relativity" has been virtual reality. The Internet is a mix of fairy tale and reality--a thing that you would neither consider a fairy tale, because it is a fairy tale, nor call reality, because it is reality.

One night I stayed at an Internet cafe. I was telling my most intimate thoughts and wishes to strangers. I felt that I would never see them and that's why I invented most of what I said.

There was a guy whose virtual name was Grigor. He wrote a ten-page letter, which he ended with words to this effect: "I hand over my letter to the internet's ocean and wait for your reply, even if you do not exist."

I replied. I probably wanted to prove my existence. He wrote again, asking me to meet him in a chat room. And then it started. Every day after ten o'clock, we would meet and chat. He said that he did not live in Armenia, that he had emigrated, and that it was important for him to spend time with Armenians.

He had become my closest friend. In the course of one month, I spent more time with him than anyone else. And then he said that he had come to Yerevan for ten days.

We decided to meet in real life. We made two appointments, but he never came.

I felt stupid. I stood in the middle of the street looking at men in the hopes of recognizing Grigor.

"What are you looking at?" It was a dickhead with pointy shoes who had covered his face with a beard to be unrecognizable. "Hey, what are you looking at?"

Thank God the city brought me home running.

A week later another guy showed up in the chat room who knew everything about me: where I go, what I do, what I wear even.

I thought Grigor had told him everything, but some time later the guy confessed that he was in fact Grigor. He said that he was born in Armenia and that he lived there, even though he hates his country, that in the last two months he has been following me, and that I know him, but of course not as Grigor.

Turns out he's gay. He likes me and he thanks fate that he was at least able to express his love virtually.

"Edi-ta," Grig let his hair down. His voice had branched out from the heat, "Edi-ta..."

"Hi," Edita's voice swam and echoed like a dial-up Internet connection.

"Hi. I didn't know you spoke Armenian."

"I... I... D... Don't know... Ar... Armenian..."

It appears that my brain was shaved along with my hair. But never mind; it's better this way. And even if it's not better, it's definitely more practical.

Edita's echo gradually faded and turned into Armenian, and the foreign girl from an unknown ethnicity began to speak in, if not literary, then at least, comprehensible Armenian.

"Heaven is somewhere around Sevan," Grig's branched-out hair wandered about in the car, "We found the place. You'll like it. Did you call Lili?"

"She's out of reach... But my message hasn't died yet."

The city was *fleeting* faster than usual. Like a gravestone, tuff-built "Yerevan" weighed down my car's breath. My city ended here. I braked.

"You haven't changed the water?" Grig knows as much about cars as I do about physics. The state of being as far from the facts as a pig pulling itself on a pull-up bar jogged memories of the woman cleaning the windows at the pharmacy, and the fish tail made itself properly felt.

"Edita is asking if there's a bathroom around here."

"What bathroom? Everything around us is a bathroom."

"I'll be right back." The branches wouldn't let Grig out of the car.

"Where are you going?"

"To the bathroom..."

I bit my tongue when I saw the funeral procession. In the past, Chopin's music was accompanied with *rabis* [20] Munchian screams.

The coffin had swaddled the deceased in such a way that his face was not visible. Only the white hair was playing with the red carnations.

At the front, two children solemnly dragged along a

---

20 Rabis is a Russian abbreviated compound form of "working-class art." Nowadays it is used derogatorily for low-class or low-brow culture, including music, dress style, and social attitudes.

youthful picture of the deceased. Behind the coffin walked the hundred-year-old widow of the deceased.

Wizened and worn from osteochondrosis, the poor wretch, holding her arms to the sky every other second, wailed:

"What did you do? Where were you going this soon? You lived a hundred and one years. Why couldn't you live another hundred and one years, eh?"

I can't say anything about an afterlife or, as the post-Soviet fashionable sufferers say, the theory of reincarnation. I basically try not to think about death. Youth gives me hope. How much time do I have until I grow old?

Apparently Grig is back in the eight-legged cage.

"Would you like a cucumber?"

"They're so big!" Edita's voice echoes and comes alive, becoming Armenian.

"Can I ask something? Why does your voice echo?"

Grig and Edita looked at each other and burst out laughing. I didn't understand whether they were laughing at what I said or at the wilted edges of the cucumbers.

"No, no, no." It's Edita. "Don't cut like that..."

"Well then how should I cut them?"

"Lengthwise, not circular..."

"What difference does it make?"

"A cucumber cut lengthwise tastes better."

The wet salt burned my tongue.

"They're nice cucumbers. We don't have cucumbers like these where I'm from..."

"And where are you from?"

"What do you do?" Tearing open the bag, Grig was filling the octopus' cage with chips.

"And where are you from?" freezes in the air and

evaporates instantly in July's heat.

"Slow-ly... Guess."

"You're an anthropologist..."

"You hit the nail on the head." Seven out of her eight legs turned into fists. "Yay..."

"Really?"

"In part... You guessed the main part, only the edges are left."

"Sociologist..."

"If I had been a sociologist, what would I be doing in your country?"

"What do you mean to say?" Grig's hair, at the possibility of winning the crown of Cilicia, turned into a chignon at the nape of his neck.

"I always thought that Armenians were like-minded."

"On what subject?"

"On all subjects; for instance, the genocide."

"Are you familiar with the issue?" Photographs of Grigor's great-grandfathers appeared in his eyes.

"Of course..."

"So?"

"I'm not a genocide expert..."

"So you're a philosopher." My car opened up a new road.

"Are you mad?"

"Why mad? A little strange..."

"No, I'm not a philosopher either... And are you a Buddhist?"

"How did you come to that? Ah, yes, from my bald head..."

"No, there's an anti-Christian glow in your eyes."

"I don't believe in the Bible," I said and got scared

that my car would lose its appetite and, unable to brake, would roll us into the valley.

"So what do you believe in?"

"Jesus."

"Are you an heretic?"

"Yeah, that's it... And I shaved my hair for another reason."

"What reason? To be sexy?"

"And what is there in my eyes?" Grig chimed in, flipping the photographs.

"I don't know..."

"No, I got tired..."

"Of taking care of your hair?"

"I got it. You're a hairdresser."

"Don't say funny things. Is there a hairdresser competition in Armenia?"

"I don't think so."

"You didn't say what's in my eyes."

"A cartoon..."

I took on my mother's scent through my sweat and sweated some more.

"You're not an artist, are you?"

"There should be artists in Armenia."

"How do you know?" It's Grig. "Who do you know?"

"No one... There's no country that doesn't have artists."

"Gagik is drawing a cartoon..."

"Really?"

"Yeah... About my mother's scent."

"That's great... I thought it'd be about Grigor."

"About Grig?"

"I'm sorry, but are you together?"

My car threw up the asphalt it had eaten.

"Are we that alike?" I braked. "I know one thing for sure: there are no gays in our country."

"Really? I remember a time when they said that there was no sex in the Soviet Union."

"Are you a sexologist?"

"You're wrong again..."

"I'd rather hang myself than sleep with a guy."

"You've never tried?"

"To sleep with a guy?" Grig was so surprised he could have shaved his head.

"To commit suicide."

"There's a text in my room: *'Ne dazhdyoshsya menya, petlya.'*"

My ears buzzed: it was probably because of all the ups and downs in the road.

"What? I didn't get it..."

I got it: the Russian language was missing from Edita's internet translator.

"And do you have girlfriends?"

"Grig didn't have one a few days ago. I introduced you to my girlfriend, Miss."

"I remember... And why 'Miss'?"

"What do you mean?"

"As soon as we started talking about your girlfriend, you immediately switched to politely calling me Miss."

"I'm sorry."

"Don't worry... We're traveling. We definitely won't get far if we address each other politely.'"

Honesty loosened my tongue. My teeth didn't get a chance to lock up my shame.

"Do you love Grig?"

Grigor's mouth dropped open and froze. In the blink of an eye, the priest cat appeared in a passing frame playing with the sun.

"No." The octopus licked the salt of the cucumber. "What made you think so?"

"I guess it just seemed to me... You split from the rest after the reception."

The cat rolled the sun's disk into the valley--the tunnel swallowed my car.

Grig's shock burned in the dark. Until the light came back, he clucked at my bald head.

"But you're really an asshole, you know?"

The tunnel, unable to digest, spat out my car.

"And so you still haven't told us what your profession is."

We were quiet until Sevan.

"The lake was wearing a blue kerchief."

Summers have a tendency to freeze.

There were three of them and then a fourth showed up. Three people were sitting at a café on the sidewalk across from the Opera. Passers-by melted in the heat and Saryan's hoary statue [21] changed its colors with the night, but they kept on sitting. Four people had frozen in the summer and remained outside of the weather.

The young lady with fruit arranged on her hat was in profile, the man with the clean-shaved head had an androgynous face, the youth wearing a black blouse with a smoke hanging from his lips had his back half-turned. Above them stood the fourth person, who, even then, I didn't understand whether he was coming or going. His

21 Martiros Saryan (1880-1972) was a famous Armenian painter. A statue of him stands in a small park across from the Opera.

white Italian hat did not match his tracksuit or the Chinese book of divination pressed under his arm.

All four of them were writers. It's hard to think that their statues will be erected after their deaths. They have frozen like statues in the summer's biography. And that, rest assured, is not something trivial.

Hearing the sentence "The lake was wearing a blue kerchief," the young lady, eating an apricot from her hat, would say, "That's not a good line. There's something *rabis* in it."

Sevan instantly gulped us down. The octopus felt like a fish in water. Grig was taking desperate measures to save her. That daughter-of-a-bitch Edita was an excellent swimmer.

"Edi-ta!" Grig wanted to find himself in the eight-legged cage again, "Wait for me!"

"Come!"

"But I don't know how to swim!"

Should I not film them? Too bad I don't have an empty tape. There was an old one. I played it to see what was on it. Grig's Ex-Girlfriend was dancing. Her red dress and bronze face appeared for a moment, and then disappeared between the running buildings. Grig's lips pressed against her lips, the frame suddenly changed, and a mouth appeared on the display. He was dripping with political intelligence. Should I erase it? No, I'll film over it.

I filmed and watched to see how it turned out.

Shot one: Edita, with her eight legs, is tightly holding onto Sevan's blue.

Shot two: Grig's branched-out hair is extending toward Edita.

Shot three: the Ex-Girlfriend sways her butt while

dancing.

Did the feeling of what I had erased have an effect on the new footage?

Shot one: Grig, his wet hair draped over his shoulders.

Shot two: (cutaway shot: a middle-aged miner with a close-up of his gold teeth.) What a hot chick... Huh, doesn't she have tits?

Shot three: Edita is pouring sand on her chest.

Shot one: close-up of Edita's lips.

Shot two: close-up of the Ex-Girlfriend's lips.

Together: mwah... mwah...

There's a few missing shots. Let me try again. It's not working. The film's ambition is probably more powerful than the footage of my inner reality.

And the Ex-Girlfriend stubbornly won't get erased.

Edita doesn't seem to want to be filmed. For a moment her mouth opened and froze when her name resounded through the loudspeaker that announces information on lost or drowned people.

"Edita, what is happiness for you?"

Extending the sixth of her eight legs, she screeched, "Don't film me! Don't!" She turned off the camera with her fingers.

REW... PLAY... The Ex-Girlfriend was painting her nails blood-red.

The loudspeaker persisted:

"Edita... What do you do to be happy?"

"Don't film, I said!"

The distorted camera was hunting down random half-orange shots of the lake on whose background, for moment, was sketched the Ex's wide-open mouth and the Munchian scream frightened at who knows what or at everything:

"Asshole... Grig, I hate you."

The loudspeaker drowned out the Girlfriend's scream and asked the third question without an answer:

"Edita, can you talk about your first love?"

The angry Octopus, letting go of Sevan's blue, yelled out:

"Don't you understand that I don't give interviews?"

The house found us on the way.

It was not a house; it was a ramshackle coach next to which was a paralyzed car serving as an attribute completing the whole. The legs and body of the coach were wrapped in merciless barbed wire and raspberry bushes. This was probably why the poor thing couldn't escape. Fine, let's say it managed to escape from its owners, where would it run? The smell of fish that came from the inside was so pungent that Edita felt compelled to douse herself with a bottle of "Poison."

There were three residents in the coach: father, mother, and son. They were fishers, all day in the sun, all day under the fire. A strange feeling enveloped me when I saw them. For five years the pain of preserving the nation had tormented me. In the beginning it expressed itself through war and the divorce of my parents, and then through famine, emigration, and my father's recited speeches at political party dinners.

But seeing the fishers, another uneasiness arose in me. Basically, if this continues, a section of the lake's population will change its race and become black.

"Feel free to come in. This house is always open to people," the fisher was doing everything he could to invite us in.

"No, no," Edita was trying to free herself from his net. "I'd like to look at your sea a little..."

"It's up to you... Would you like some jam? We just made some... Wife, bring the jam."

"Sure, I'll eat some," the glutton Grig immediately chimed in, "but in about five minutes. Can I come in?"

"Come in, brother, this is a house... Make yourself at home."

My heart sank. I'm twenty-one, but I've never felt at home in this city.

"How old are you?" The woman extended a plate of blood-red raspberries to Edita.

"Thirty-two..."

"That's a good age... I'm two years older than you."

"What about..." one of the raspberries got stuck on Edita's chin, "what about your son?"

"My Valodik? He turned sixteen this year."

"It's a beautiful cross..."

"Yes... It's from my christening. And you don't have a cross? You probably don't like to wear it, do you?"

"I don't know... I guess..."

"Are you married to the one with long hair?"

"What?"

"Do you have any children?"

"Not yet... We're like a married couple, but..."

"I get it... Would you like some more jam?"

Holding in my laugh somehow, I went into the house.

"Grig, you'll die when I tell you this... Grig?"

Grig had buried himself in the bed and was twitching like a fish. Something familiar was spread at the head of the bed. It was a flowery cloth--you don't come across many of those now.

Grig ignored me. He got up and said "Where's the jam? Bring it!" and went out of the coach.

The flowery cloth remained at the head of the bed.

"Send your son to Yerevan. We'll make sure he gets into college." Grigor, lapping up the raspberry, was dispensing his royal generosity.

"What?" The fisher almost boxed Valodik's ear upon hearing the word "college." "No college! A better place than this? Let him learn..."

"What is he supposed to learn here?"

"To catch fish. He'll look after his family and himself better than any one of those college graduates."

"And what if the lake runs out of fish?"

"It won't..."

"How do you know? Sevan is drying up..."

"On the contrary, it's filling up. There's a God above."

"Sure..." The Cilicia crown became a chignon again at the nape of Grigor's neck. "Now that you said God, I remembered. Isn't there a place called 'Heaven's Door' around here?"

"No idea."

"Isn't it near the church?"

"I know that area well. It's definitely not around the monastery."

Grig got up hopelessly and went to the spring. He took off his pants and put on wide shorts. For a moment I imagined him butt-naked wearing only a tailcoat, and for a split second the Ex-Girlfriend appeared in a cutaway shot.

"Asshole!" The Munchian mouth was devouring the camera. "Grig, I hate you."

When he got up to wash the bowl of jam, his testicles appeared. I rubbed my eyeballs to dispel the sighting.

The Girlfriend got erased, but the testicles were still visible. Idiot. I walked over to cover the disgraceful sight with my body when I heard the fisher's wife's voice from the coach. Even though she only spoke with a whisper, her mythologically emotional voice thundered and spread all over the Geghama mountains.

"Valodik, aren't you ashamed? Why is your flowery underwear spread on the bed?"

In slow motion, Grig's right hand stretched out to obscure the sun and his left ordered us to retreat. For a moment the car stood up, attempted to throw off the barbed wire, but defeated, found itself thoroughly painted with the red of the raspberries. The seconds flew by in fast-forward. My car, without properly wishing anyone well, stole us away, leaving the empty bottle of "Poison" in the fisher's wife's hand.

I like balls a lot. I love all of the ways it manifests itself and flies, except for one. I know that some people will push the label humanism on it, but I really don't like the fact that, in Armenian, a synonym of the word "bullet" is ball.

To me, the ball finds its full expression in football, even though the first time I got the idea of a "ball" was in another game.

Until I was a teenager, we often played Gortsagorts--a mispronunciation of Russian "gorod za gorod," meaning "city to city." At that time I didn't know where that strange word had come from. It seemed to me that it had something to do with knitting and braiding. [22] You knitted one person into another with a ball and at the same time

22 In Armenian, gortsagorts is close in meaning to "knitting and braiding."

you made a third a victim through the imaginary braid.

We didn't get to enter the church.

The road seemed knitted and braided.

The jump cuts moved the church to and from us. It was now under our noses, not even three or four meters away, and now far from us, making only its cupola worthy to our eyes. We skipped from one part of the road to the next, but still didn't manage to reach our destination.

My car merged from one highway to the next for ten, fifteen minutes, and then, exhausted, it unexpectedly skidded, tore apart the blue of Sevan, and braked near Moscow Cinema. [23]

In the blink of an eye, a red carpet rolled out to the mouth of the building, and the breath and smacking lips of the ruler of the Soviet Union thirty years ago could be felt through the loudspeaker as they announced the opening of the festival. After the priest's breathless blessing--the poor thing probably didn't know there were erotic films in the festival's program--and after the actors had played theatrical passages and danced the Kochari [24] like animals that don't even exist, the solemn time had come for the honorable guests and participants to pass over the carpet. However, two representatives of our country, who swear they have received international recognition as artists, had barely had a chance to set foot on the red when a brass band raised such a clamor that the rest of the participants, afraid to lose their hearing, rushed into the building.

The most unfortunate, naturally, were the talented

------

23 Moscow Cinema is a movie theater in Yerevan that has hosted the opening of the Golden Apricot International Film Festival every year since its inception in 2004.
24 The Kochari is a traditional Armenian folk dance.

ones who appeared at the end and didn't manage to get in. Ten minutes later a street-sweeping water truck flooded the courtyard of the theater with a strange yellow solution. The organizers of the festival, leaving behind their guests, tried to convince the driver to at least postpone his duty by an hour. However, the driver was unflinching, because he had to be home at exactly eight o'clock so that he could watch the 585th episode of a thousand-episode Venezuelan show.

Summers had a tendency to move around statues.

It was those four from the café who had been brought and made to stand in front of Moscow Cinema on the other side of the crowd control barricades.

The girl, who had by now eaten and finished all the fruit on her hat, was keeping herself busy with Chinese divination. The man with the Italian hat extended his right hand to the hovering girl whose sky-blue hair had spread out and was flown over the red carpet in slow-motion. Only sometimes, sometimes did the tips of her toes brush the ground, leaving traces of washing powder on the red.

The other two were standing face-to-face smoking and talking. It looked like they'd run out of breath if they started talking without cigarettes.

"Don't you want to quit smoking?" The young man with the androgynous face asked.

"I quit, eh... And you?"

"I don't smoke at home. I only feel the need when I'm around people."

"Wouldn't it be better if you didn't see anyone?"

"Probably... Not only will my lungs be spared, but so will..."

Four people had frozen in the summer time and had been left out of the seasonal festival. The music and color of the city changed with the light, but they, they were standing, and as such they didn't see a single film.

Edita was unable to enter the hotel--the red carpet was closing off her path.

When the roar of the brass band ended, Yerevan's wind embraced the festival in its whirl. Countless plastic bottles and colorful pieces of paper like postcards addressed to the world circled the air, flew up and away.

In slow-motion, the wind stopped for a moment choking in dust, after which the seconds flew in fast-forward.

The eight-legged woman straddled the red carpet and flew over Yerevan's night.

With my eyes still closed, I relived the summer. The heat was in my blood. And as luck would have it, in the last two days, the red was not moving below the 43rd line on the thermometer scale. There was no point in thinking about the black, especially after yesterday's adventures in Sevan. With purple strokes in my head, I jumped up and drew the curtain.

The smell of lahmajoon was spiced with my mother's fresh scent. I lit a cigarette. I had forgotten to turn off the buzz of my phone. No one had called. It was the third day that my battery needed to regain consciousness.

Mom? My mom's scent really was fresh. I roamed around the house trying to find the source. I finally found it. The scent was coming off a piece of paper:

"My dear Gagik, where are you hanging out? I found out that you had gone to your grandmother's. And you've turned off your phone. Or are you out of reach? I'm leaving. Not for long. Only for two days. There are cutlets in the fridge. Don't forget to eat them. You haven't lost any weight, have you? Your mother..."

The scent was unbearable. I have to go back to the village, to my grandmother's house. Mom, do you remember? You couldn't stand the summers. You would suffocate.

Three people lived in the apartment on the third floor: the Old Woman, the Spinster, and an Unknown person sitting on a bed. Once a week, the relatives of the Unknown person would bring food for the house-owners as barter for living there.

In the summers, they would leave the door of their apartment open. I don't know what they cooked or did, but the building took on such an inhuman stench that we would go up and down holding our noses.

Only one section of the apartment was visible from the outside. The closed door of the living-room, the bed in the kitchen--which, besides the Unknown woman, had taken upon its shoulders a mattress and blanket sick with jaundice--an old lamp, and an aloe plant that was growing in an olive oil container. The wind played with the formerly white nylon curtains and filled the room every now and again with crazy--from the smell?--swarms of moths.

Sometimes they would also leave the bathroom door open, which blocked my vision to the depths of the apartment and served to spread new, inhuman smells to the stairwell.

The Spinster wasn't visible. One time I only saw her hand wearing a whorish cuff from the times of Noah. It was feeding the Unknown woman who had her eyes closed.

The portrait of the Spinster in the hall constantly changed her facial expression and sometimes even took on a moustache and beard. In moments like these, she was probably thinking about men or recalling her father.

The door of the living-room was always closed. As they say: God, deliver us from evil.

I was going up one day when the door opened and the old owner appeared in the stairwell wearing a thousand-year-old kimono worthy of being in the Chinese National History Museum. What do you want me to say? I could even point out the color of her menstrual tsunami...

"It's unbearable," I took on my mother's scent through my sweat and sweated some more. "Gagik, do something, I can't stand those smells anymore... I'm suffocating..."

There was a time when I wanted to make a film about them. Nothing absurd, not even using special lighting. Each time I went up or down, with a camera in my hand, I would film a few second of their floor for a month. I wouldn't even need to edit. Nor have music--the muddled radio announced the women's thoughts.

I thought about it, but didn't film. What I had seen was probably more powerful than anything I'd film.

Lili was out of reach. I don't understand Italian, but from the bel canto of the answering machine, I figured that they were staying with Davit.

My text message was still dead. I turned off my phone thinking about the witch mother for the first time in six months.

There were red specks on the morning.

My grandmother's hair opened the gate.

"Bless you, my dears," she kissed Edita and Grig, poured a bucket of feed in the pig bowl, and embraced my head with her armpit hair. "Is your mother wandering abroad again?"

"Grandma, these are my friends..."

"Bless you, my dears..."

The similarity between the legs of the house and my grandmother's hair had grown deeper. I recalled the noise of the city and my antennas compressed by the wind, and I shuddered. My grandmother would not be able to stand Yerevan's lead. She would go crazy.

"If you shaved her hair, it would turn into giant blond crosses."

For a split second, in a cutaway shot, the statues of the summer appeared and the girl with the fruit lined up on her hat was thoroughly patronizing:

"What would it turn into? *Crosses?* That's not a good line. There's something *rabis* in it."

In the last ten days her hair had changed a lot. They had branched out somehow or, more precisely, they had become rooted. My poor grandmother didn't have a job, and now she was forced to drag around those rough and heavy roots.

A woodpecker had appeared on her right temple driving everyone crazy with its ticking. In general, the hair had somehow gotten heavier, sweeping and emptying with more difficulty. When it finally lit the fireplace, my grandmother was exhausted.

"Bless you, my dears, what can I make? Should I slaughter a lamb?"

"Grandma, we're not hungry. We came to see you and go. How are you?"

"I'm fine, I'm fine." A clump of dry hair broke off while throwing wood in the fire. "It's nothing... It's just hair... It's just grown so long, it's tiring."

"Grandma, leave it, I'll do it..."

"So you finally shaved your head, did you?" The hair stroked my bald head.

"Yeah, I don't want your neighbors to gossip..."

"What neighbors? There's no one left. The last time it was me who shaved your head..."

"When?"

"You were five," the hair started to pluck the chicken...

"Grandma, how are the sparrows?"

"Two of the chicks died..."

My uncle's thirty-year-old accusing-forgiving smile drew open the curtain of my childhood. Genderless and transparent toys began to spin around the room. I sweated. The smell of my armpits reprinted Gagik's face and dislocated his facial features and limbs. When his beard appeared instead of his eyes, my mother's scent became unbearable:

"The older you get, the more you take after Grandpa Paryur," the voice resounded in my ears and a red sparrow flew out of my uncle's mouth.

"I'll call him Gagik!" the picture screamed and froze.

Traces of kisses appeared on his face. At that moment, he was probably thinking about the girl he loved.

What should we call him?

"Gagik?" Edita threw the toys out of the window. "There are so many mosquitoes!"

The smile on my uncle's face was a regular smile.

"Who is it?"

"Gagik."

"Your grandfather?"

"My uncle. I was born when he died. They called me Gagik in his honor."

"Okay... And that's why you can't forgive..."

"Who?"

"The sparrows are nice..."

"Who can I not forgive?"

Edita held her head with six legs.

"Do you know?" Did she start speaking in literary language? "There comes a time after you turn thirty when you understand that you cannot forgive your relatives. My closest relatives after my parents are my grandfathers. I haven't seen either of them. They died long ago. Can you believe it? I cannot forgive the dead."

"What have they done that you can't forgive them?"

"I forget how I got hurt by meeting people. I'll get annoyed and won't meet that person for a month or a year, and I'll suffer. I need to see the person and talk to them to be able to forgive them. I forgave my parents by talking to them..."

"What did your grandfathers do that you can't forgive them?"

"Who asked them to give birth to me?"

My grandmother's hair entered the room and took four glasses from the cupboard. The gurgling of the wine gathered us around the table.

"It's not wine; it's blood, blood," Grig, holding the belly of the bottle, was arranging the glasses.

"I'm not drinking," my eyes began to sweat.

"Why not?"

"Aren't I driving?" Images of my mother refused to disappear.

"Will you let me braid your hair?" Edita instantly set to work.

"No, leave it, bless you, leave it," my grandmother, feeling embarrassed, spread her hair on the floor. "I'll be lost if you imprison this, too..."

"Grandma, is neighbor Hambo's house still here?"

"It is. Of course it is... No one lives there... The son locked it up and left..."

"Do you remember that we were in Hambo's basement when I got the mumps?"

My grandmother's hair felt dismayed.

"I remember. Of course I remember, how can I not?"

"Grandma, it always seemed to me that I got it from pulling on the tail of a pig."

"No, son... It wasn't from that..."

"Then what was it from, grandma?"

"I don't know... When you were little and I would tell you about King Tiridates [25] and you would get very scared..."

"What king?" Edita was devouring the chicken wings.

"Nothing... My uncle died in the war."

"Which one?" Edita's question, taking on mythological dimensions, thundered in the nearby mountains, horrifying the soldiers sleeping in the observation posts, and died down in the wine glass. "Okay, I got it..."

"Grandma, you have red specks on your face..."

For the first time I saw that my grandmother's face was very young, that it hadn't changed since she was a girl.

"What is there over there?" Edita lit a smoke. "There, on the other side of the valley..."

---

25 King Tiridates was a fourth century Armenian king who converted Armenia to Christianity after Saint Grigor the Illuminator cured him of his madness. During his madness, King Tiridates believed that he had turned into a boar.

"There's nothing. There's Turks..."

The pigs, hearing the word Turk, pushed the door of the gate and went in.

My tongue tied.

In slow-motion, my grandmother's hair drove out the pigs with a stick. For a moment my uncle's face thought about his loved one, after which the seconds fast-forwarded by, flying us over the church on the mountain.

My grandmother's hair stayed behind on the crossed open gate.

Her final words were tied to the back of my car like ribbons:

"Take good care of that child..."

August has become a prostitute.

Grig found himself in Edita's room by chance--he had lost his comb. The heat, which had broken down the border between the inside and outside, was making Edita cry.

Grig asked why she was crying. The woman said it was the heat and lit a cigarette. Then, after thrusting the cigarette in the throat of an ashtray, she took off her shirt, sat down, and continued to smoke. Grigor approached her. He leaned against the bed and kissed Edita's mouth. Edita continued to smoke. He kissed her again, stroked her teeth with his tongue, and probably felt white delicacies in her mouth.

"How much you like to kiss!" she said and tore open the buttons of Grig's jeans. He was in his swimming trunks. She lowered those, too. His penis was big and thick. "It's thick..."

"Don't worry," Grig's hair branched out involuntarily, "no one has died from it yet..."

In slow-motion, the condom slipped out of my pocket, walked on its own feet and fell into Grig's hand.

With his right hand, the man pushed away the heavy paws of the curtain on the woman's breasts, and with his left he leaned against the bed and penetrated. The seconds flew by in fast-forward. Grig and Edita spun around the room like fluff in a whirlwind.

"Asshole! Grig, I hate you," the Ex-Girlfriend was becoming mercilessly erased.

For a moment the summer statues appeared in the whirlwind and when it was time for oral sex, the watermelon on the girl's hat tipped over and left red traces on the walls.

"Those are cool lines. There's nothing *rabis* about them..."

The seconds slowed down again for a moment. And then everything settled.

Edita puffed up her eight legs and spat out Grig. The tail that had grown out of the man's penis flung him into the swimming pool.

Grig, with the needles of the water on his back, appeared in front of my face.

"You're not swimming?"

"No," my stomach was churning. I was very close to biting his nose out of anger.

"Why?"

"I don't have trunks..."

"Neither do I." I only noticed the flapping shark tail just now. "Come, don't be embarrassed... There's no one around besides Edita..."

My mother's scent would not get out of me. I drowned.

The blades of the water scratched my eyes and slashed the old protesting woman's face. For a moment only her mouth remained, open and frozen on the lousy tricolor flag:

"Damn you, aren't you supposed to be the youth of this nation?"

With air in my lungs and my nose in Grig's round and white behind, I swam from one end to the other. I came and went once or twice not paying attention to the flapping of my tail. The idiot's thick penis was playing in the water. Compared to his, mine was teeny-weeny, kind of like an almond...

The wet, branched-out hair sprawled on Grigor's face.

"What smell is this?"

There was a scar on his back from the time he got struck by a knife. In my head, I also struck him. His foot slipped and he sprawled on the edge of the pool. The Munchian scream was imprinted in my head. My father's, my mother's, and God knows who else's pictures turned their faces to the wall... Now I told you why you should turn...

Grigor leaned on the mouth of the pool with his arms and slipped into the water looking into my eyes.

"There's a wound on your nose," he said, beating the water with his legs.

"How's Edita?"

"What are you trying to say?"

"You get it or what?"

"Why did you let me get out of the water?"

"I don't get it..."

"Gag, aren't you killing me?"

The silent Munchian scream raised a second wave of despair and my phone chirped...

It was Lili--she had sent a message. My phone tried to fly away from my wet fingers twice.

I opened the message. The horned and tailed letters devoured my eyes.

"Gag, mom wasn't feeling bad... Grig asked me to get dirty with him and I did... I'm sorry... Bye... Or take care. LILI"

I don't want to die... Dying is harder than living.

Lili was rubbing her vagina. She would stretch her underwear with her fingers, pull it down, stroke it with her palm, bear it for a moment, then not bear it any longer, and rub again.

From the look on her witch mother's face that had appeared in close-up, I got that she was having her period. Her broken-out face rippled from the crimson tsunami.

My sweat pissed out like a shower. The scent was pouring out of me and would not come to an end. My nose and mouth, my ears, my skin, and my stomach were all filled with my mother's putrid stench.

Message, you were dead--couldn't you have stayed dead? For ten days I didn't know that Lili wasn't mine.

Idiot. Idiot. I thought Grig had taken Edita that night to fuck...

The bitch was rubbing her vagina, probably preparing to do somersaults on Davit's penis.

Tree, I bear your pain...

For a moment I considered crashing my car against the tree, to get my mother's scent out of me and die, but I changed my mind. How is the tree to blame? Without this, those wretches are already oppressed so much, uprooted, cut, made into paper, and taken into bathrooms.

Grig's ass was playing in front of my face: round, white, hairless.

"Asshole, Grig, I hate you!"

The camera was hardly coquettish: it turned on instantly and shoved the footage in my face.

Shot one: Grig, his wet hair draped over his shoulders.

Shot two: (cutaway shot: a middle-aged miner with a close-up of his gold teeth.) What a hot chick... Eh, doesn't she have tits?

Shot three: the text of the dead message...

The end. The movie ended.

In anger, my car turned its wheels only twice before plumping itself in front of Yerevan Cinema.

My father's hand and his gray-specked beard, which resembled the melting peak of Ararat, appeared somewhere between the wine glass and the condom.

"What are you drinking?" He picked up the glass and took a sip. "Is your mother here?"

"She left two days ago."

"Where to?"

"I don't know. She didn't say..."

"All right. You don't come around. Your sister is asking about you all the time. At least call."

"I'll call..."

"Take good care of your mother," he said, shoving his index finger and middle finger in my belt. "You've lost weight..."

"Did the president like the restaurant?"

"Very much, but he couldn't stay more than half an hour. He had a meeting. You'll take good care of yourself, right? Don't drink too much..."

He left, wiping his dripping beard.

There's a strange landscape-looking restaurant close to the cinema. Every night Mother Armenia--the statue-

-digs a hole for herself and crawls into it in shame of the toasts and patriotic slogans. Twice she swung her sword like a samurai and almost cut the landscape of the restaurant in half, but at the very last moment maternity played inside of her and both times her strikes fell on Grandpa Lenin's bird-shat head instead.

My father's beard had completely melted. Longing for Ararat, he poured a few glasses down his throat and began to sing.

I remembered the asshole with the crooked neck and crooked legs who called me "son of a bitch," and Yerevan's lead boiled in me. I wanted to talk to someone. I collected my sister's number.

"Hello... Who's this?"

"It's me..."

"Gagik?" She started to cry. "How are you?"

"I'm fine and you?"

"I'm not okay... I was beaten..."

"Who beat you?"

"Your father... He caught me ten days ago with my boyfriend and beat me with a broom. I have scars on my face... Gag, I love you very much..."

"We'll see each other in two days..."

"Gag?"

My father's picture, which was cut out of the newspaper, was giving a speech on the fight against corruption. Next to me, two rotten mouths froze on the lousy tricolor flag.

"He's given his life to the homeland. Shouldn't he have done that? He has a family to look after..."

In slow-motion, the butterfly condom flew out of my pocket and landed on my index finger. I extended my right hand and held onto the Araratian beard, and... The seconds flew by in fast-forward smacking the slimy rubber entity onto my father's hand.

Run, city, run.

My car held its breath and flew through the Versailles that had been built by a benefactress. The Greek gods and tripterous angels flooded the sky.

The wings of one of them had broken off. It was flapping on the asphalt when the head of a bull fenced in a Hummer drove over it. I pulled it away and blocked him. Lili rubbed her vagina at the bull's bellow.

My blood made me take on my mother's scent...

Run, city, run...

"Dear Gagik, where are you hanging out? I found out that you had gone to your grandmother's. And you've turned off your phone. Or are you out of reach? I'm leaving. Not for long. Only for two days. There are cutlets in the fridge. Don't forget to eat them. You haven't lost any weight, have you? Your mother..."

My mother's scent flooded the house. I can't stand it, I'm suffocating.

I don't know whether I heard or read that in order to protect your house from scorpions you have to burn one of them.

The text message was burning with a scream. My father's, my mother's, and God knows who else's pictures turned their faces to the wall in shame.

I opened the mouth of the closet, took out my mother's clothes, poured gasoline on them, and set them on fire.

Pictures, you don't want to see fire, eh? You'll see... I forcefully turned back their snouts.

The smoke was suffocating.

For a moment, by the outside door, I saw the hand of the Spinster who lived on the second floor with a whorish cuff from the times of Noah.

"What are you doing?" Her voice was deep--she was probably thinking about men. "Gagik, do something. We can't take the smells of your house anymore... We're suffocating..."

Run, city, run...

My sister's number was violating my phone. I would turn it off and she would call again. I picked up to say a few sweet words to her as well...

Her voice gushed out at once...

"Gagik? Gag, grandma died..."

My grandmother's body was put in the courtyard because she didn't have a house.

My father's mouth had stayed open and frozen on the pall when a phalanx of journalists stormed around him.

"Please accept our condolences..."

"Thank you..."

"I know that this is not the best time to ask, but, nevertheless, how are you feeling?"

"Better already... Though worse at the same time..."

"Has your mother ever been a symbol of the Homeland for you?"

"My mother was everything for me: my homeland, my past, my childhood..."

"How, or with what methods, did your mother sow love for the homeland? Through fairy tales?"

"I was never told fairy tales. The only fairy tales I got were the carvings of the church on the mountain. And an animated film was shown at our village club once. Me and my two brothers competed against each other repeating 'cartoon, cartoon, cartoon' as fast as we could without taking a breath. Whoever said 'cartoon' the most without taking a breath won."

"If I'm not mistaken, your mother used to be a teacher. What influence did school have on you?"

"My mother was a life teacher. She was almost illiterate, but she was a wise woman. As for school, I only remember everything until fourth grade. Soviet schooling left a bad impression on me. It was uninteresting. Fourth grade was the best."

"Do you agree with the saying that a mother is the hearth of the home?"

"Absolutely. My mother was bread; she was a bread-giver. She beat me only once. I remember. It was summer. My neighbor's daughter was called home and beaten with a broom. I don't remember now why it happened. To this day I feel guilt. And the girl left for America long ago."

"What did your mother do when you went to war? Did she ever try to stop you?"

"The war happened in our courtyard. My brother died right here in front of the gate. The first time I went up to the trenches, she said: 'Rely only on yourself.' I don't remember where we were. They were bombing houses. There was no place to sleep. There were only a few sleeping places. My friend, who was a Kamaz driver, said: 'Don't worry, you'll stay with me.' When everyone had found a place, I went up to my friend and he said: 'Sorry, I can't put you up. The boys of our battalion are here.' I was standing under the black sky and there was an enormous valley in front of me. I was alone, I was so alone that the mountains thundered with every breath I took. From that day on I swore to only rely on myself. That's probably the reason why I'm still alive today..."

"And what about your son? Will he continue your work?"

My grandmother had decided to wash her head.

The hair had taken a pot from the basement and filled it with water. Noise had come from the house as a fire was being lit. She had driven away the woodpecker that was on her temple and gone into the living-room. She had sat down, taken out the notebook with stories about people she had lost, and read it.

In the course this, my uncle's portrait had smiled a couple of times. My grandmother's hair had stood on end in fear. I don't know, but she probably ate the pages of the notebook to overcome the fear. And then she left the room with a brush in her hand.

The fire was extinguishing. Her hair had caught fire while throwing wood in the wood stove. She had tipped over the pot. She had sat on the floor for two minutes, then she had gotten up to get scissors to cut off the burned parts of her hair, but she had not been able to move. The root hairs had dug into the ground and frozen. Imprisoned by her real hair, my grandmother had moved left and right, her hand had extended to get the ax and... A heart attack had devoured my grandmother's heart.

With her hair in the ground, wrapped around the grapevines and the handles of the gates, she had tried to scream, to call for help, but she had felt her hairy throbbing body in her throat.

When she died, a red sparrow flew out of her mouth.

My grandmother's body was put in the courtyard because she didn't have a house.

The legs of the house had opened up right after her death...

We searched for five days, but couldn't find my grandmother's *fleeted* house...

Grig's shitty snout was circling under my nose. He tried to approach me a few time, probably to give his condolences, but I didn't let him.

Edita, with her octopus look, was urging the youth to sit on chairs with their legs crossed. Alas the chairs that the neighbors had brought from their homes were electric. No one could stand them for more than five minutes.

The record was half an hour, which was set by the neighbor's eighteen-year-old grandson. It's also true that in that half hour he had to change his pants three times.

One of the wrinkled mouths of the old grieving women stayed open and frozen on the white cloth covering the mirror.

"What have you done?" she was addressing my grandmother. "You lived this long. Why couldn't you live as long?" Holding the woman by her armpits, the neighbors brought her out of the gate. When she passed by Edita, she murmured under her breath: "Damn you, aren't you supposed to be the youth of this nation?"

I didn't see my sister's face. She was leaning on my shoulder and crying. Grig, taking advantage of the situation, walked up, offered his condolences, and held his hand out to me.

"I'm sorry..."

My sister tightly hugged Grig and walked to my grandmother.

"Gag..."

"Why did you bring Edita?"

"Now is not the time for that... She wanted to come..."

"And when is the time for that?"

"One day when..."

"Grig, are you crazy? What are you hoping for? My kindness? I don't want to see you ever again."

"Gag, I'll tell you, you'll understand..."

"What are you going to tell me? How you fucked Lili?"

"Gag?"

"At least have some decency. It's my grandmother's funeral and you talk about sex... Now is not the time for that..."

My mother did not come to the funeral. She was not in the city or, more precisely, in the country.

Her faded scent wandered in the house. The pictures had become distorted--they were probably ashamed to learn.

The scent emanated from the paper.

"Gagik, I cried when I saw the burned clothes. No, I'm not sorry for my clothes, even though there were a few Versaces among them.

Dear Gagik... I understood that you, too, are of their burning kin...

Take good care of yourself. I don't know when I'll return... I might get married... Your mother..."

It's unbearable, I can't stand the smells anymore... I'm suffocating!

The door of the second-floor apartment was closed.

A week ago, the three of them--the Old House-Owner, the Spinster, and the Unknown woman who had gotten out of bed--went to a funeral.

The one who drowned was one of the fishers from Sevan. With his wife and son, who carried the name Valodik, he lived in a ramshackle coach next to which, as an attribute completing the whole, was a paralyzed car.

The father dreamed of his son becoming a fisher and supporting his family. The son dreamed of studying in the city and looking at pictures of naked women.

The coach had never seen this many people. Unable to bear the sight of the mourners, the poor thing had collapsed.

The Spinster remained in the coach. The Old House-Owner, as became apparent later, drowned in the Sevan. As for the Unknown woman's fate, no one ever found out. After searching for a week, the Unknown woman was listed as a person missing without a trace.

Valodik did not wait long. Scared of the collapsing coach, the paralyzed car unfastened itself, parted the blue of the Sevan, and brought him to Yerevan.

I was in the stairwell when the Ex-Girlfriend, not paying attention to me, opened the door of the second-floor apartment with a key.

"Asshole, Grig, I hate you!"

I walked out of the entrance and saw that nothing had remained of Yerevan. My house had *fleeted* from Abovian Street and had found itself in an unknown place. My heart sank... I'm twenty-one, but I've never felt at home in this city.

Again the word *fleet* seemed strange. But my head couldn't find an alternative... I was compelled to repeat what I had known for a long time:

I live in a *fleeting* city...

"I LIVE IN A FLEETING CITY...

The word fleeting seemed strange just now. Am I wrong? How can letters come together like that and make my city fleet? I repeat-

*ed the word a few times, scribbled it on a piece of paper, and under-
stood that to describe Yerevan, the word fleet also fleets. ."*

My mother always said that my ancestors owned great estates in Western Armenia. Many of them were killed during the Genocide. Should justice be served and we get our share of lands back, it's very possible that I will be proclaimed the prince of Cilicia...

...I see suicide as being an escape from one reality to another where it's almost the same reality as here.

...Everyone writes about their room in their own words:

Ne dazhdyoshsya menya, petlya...

"Thank you, Grigor, for the interesting conversation... And we will meet again after the commercial break."

With beautiful eyes like a foal, with tousled hair, and with one-inch long eyelashes, Gagik's pop art face appeared on the TV screen. I don't know who filmed this commercial. It's a rock-singing bird with a guitar under its arm that they throw shoes at and make fly at the end. I liked it a lot, and for a month I thought about who the animated bird looked like. In the end, I figured that something about it looked like Gagik.

"Do you see Gagik..." the reporter practically threw herself on me "...filming a cartoon? He said he was, but I don't remember what it was about."

"I'll be seeing him. We've decided to go to Sevan. I got a message early this morning. He wrote that he was living in a *fleeting* city."

"He's an interesting guy..."

"For the girls, yes... Everyone's mad about him."

"Really? But I'm interested in other kinds of guys. Is Nana also going to Sevan?"

"No... She has a show."

"Grigor, I forgot to tell you: I recorded your interview so that it can be aired a few times on the radio as well... The city leaves a static--frozen even--impression on me. There's no movement. You want coffee?"

I drop coffee in the cezve [26] and boil it for twenty minutes. The rock makes my tongue tingle and burn. I read Gagik's message again, not forgetting to pour the boiling liquid down my throat.

I'm turning thirty-one in the winter. If I weren't born in December, I would hate that month. I live in the summer and listen to rock in the winter. Sometimes I take it too far and lie down in a fever. But if I don't listen to it, I won't be able to stand the cold.

Time doesn't suffice after thirty. There are so many things tied to your neck--people included--that you don't have time to manage everything. Imagine becoming close to four people a year. You have to feed each one of them with energy, right?

Thirty is the beginning of a slow suicide, and if you *fleet* from that at the same time and...

Gagik himself is *fleeting,* but he's blaming the city. How can the city move when the citizen--in this case, Gagik--is static on the inside?

When was it? Gagik and I had gone to Sevan for a day. Nana hadn't come; she had a show.

"Slow down... Gag, are you doing it on purpose?"

"How's your dog?"

"There's no dog... I have a cat now..."

---

26 Special pot used for cooking Middle-Eastern coffee.

"Isn't a cat more dangerous? If you leave it hungry for a day, it'll jump and gouge your eyes out."

"Gag, I want to buy flowers for Nana..."

"Let's buy some..."

In five or six places my eyes fell on withered flower baskets.

"Stop. Let me get out..."

I got out... There was a bridal Mercedes five meters away. It was so mangled that it had almost completely lost its whiteness. Next to the car were green and yellow women's shoes facing each other...

I'm not a scaredy cat, but speed and dogs terrify me. Gagik is always making fun me and then one day--he had just broken up with Nana--he came and said:

"I figured out what needs to be done."

He brought me to a psychologist.

The hallway that stretches to the psychologist is end-less...

The place is familiar to me. The last time I was here was when I was serving in the army. The year is unknown, but the day was definitely Wednesday. No entry? I'm kidding. There's entry. It's just that they've put up a sign like that. There was no sign?

Those present were army bulls--cattle with hollow skulls filled with stories about chicks. They cursed every other second, as if they were in a swearing competition. They surrounded me and started laughing at me. Did I get scared? I knew that I was playing with fire. In the beginning I defended myself with jokes, but...

"Hey," my nose bled at the chief bull's bellow, "you think you're a good guy? Bring me a broom..."

A commotion broke out that only ended when the

broom appeared. They brought the broom solemnly, upholding all the subtleties of a ritual. I broke. It was impossible to pick up all the pieces, but I took the broom and started to sweep.

"Sweep well." I couldn't see the bull. His voice caused a short circuit in my ears. "He wants you to piss blood. Either way you'll have to clean it up. Or do you not know who we are?"

The hallway is endless. I'm fleeing from the war, the idiots, the blood from my nose.

Even if a thousand years went by, I wouldn't be able to erase these images from my head...

Snrk... I snorted...

I'm gasping. I hate this restaurant. It's across the cinema. Even in our city there's nothing this tasteless. It's a crude construction decorated on the outside with eagles and stones. The snow of Mount Ararat, which had been planted on the roof, was melting and rolling down like piss.

It was a banquet. The president's wife, who was standing by the door, ordered the bodyguard to let me in with a doe-like hand gesture.

"Are there many people?"

"No, just us. The president just left. When did you get back from Sevan?"

"A week ago... on Wednesday..."

"We get together every Wednesday, but today is a special occasion..."

She was a beautiful woman. She had a sharp, gentle jaw, and eyes with inch-long eyelashes. She was wearing a dress with gray polka dots. And her shoes were very thin heels.

As it turned out, the president was awarded a medal "For Courage." In turn, the guests drank toasts to him. The president's face was dark or, more precisely, green. Something was sparkling in his hand. I looked attentively: it was a condom with a transparent sheath.

The guests buried the government official who had been awarded the medal "For Courage" in gifts that they had brought.

I was looking to my left and right when I saw Nana. She was turning all the men's penises into stone with her Medusan gaze.

I had no desire to speak with her...

"Grig? You don't say hi anymore?"

"Hi..."

"I heard you got married..."

"I get the impression that the entire nation is thinking about getting me married."

"Why are you surprised? It's from you, no, that our future crown royalty will be born?"

"A year ago it could've even been from you..."

"Are you looking for Gagik?" She cut me off and with that stopped my nose from bleeding.

"No..."

"We get together every Wednesday. Will you come?"

"I don't know the location..."

"Ask your lover, she'll tell you..."

I wanted to ask what lover when she handed over a package.

"You didn't bring a present? Ay, ay, ay, aren't you ashamed? I have two gifts. I'll give you one."

"It's okay," the Medusan Viagra started to take effect.

"Take it..."

There was nothing about the box that made it stand out.

I walked up to the president. He looked sadly into my eyes and shouted:

"What's happening here? Bring whatever you were supposed to bring!"

Barbecued deer was brought. The guests greedily attacked and started to devour the animal that had been cooked with sweet peppers and tomatoes.

I was starving. I pulled off a bite from the deer's neck. The beast fluttered in such a way that it seemed alive. I hadn't gotten around to chewing anything when the president sent someone after me.

"Have you seen Gagik?" His eyes were yellow and he was speaking loudly.

"An hour ago. We went to the pool together. Then he suddenly disappeared."

"Have you seen Gagik?"

"An hour... I haven't seen him."

"And why?"

"Gagik is my friend, but I'm embarrassed to talk to him about that."

"Is this your gift?"

"Yes..."

"You know, don't you, that according to etiquette, gifts are opened when they are received?"

He crumpled the gold, crinkly paper and tore it open. My nose started to bleed. The antlers of a deer rocked in the minister's hands. He started to prance around holding the antlers to his head. And then, unexpectedly, he stood up and shouted:

"I knew it, I knew you were a bastard and that you

would disgrace me like this in the end..."

The meat froze in the throats of the gluttons. The cute faces of the women resembled the snouts of does at that moment. The minister stuck the safeguard in his hand to his forehead, put his other hand in his pocket, took out a gun, brought it up to his temple and, ignoring his wife's pleas, started to shoot, shoot, shoot...

The heavy metal of System of a Down sizzled in my ears and my thirtieth year came back again. The desire to love Nana rose in me. I wanted to take back the time I had spent with her, but the screaming and shouting made me realize that this was not the best time for that.

The woman had frozen. The freeze didn't last long. She assaulted me and cried:

"Well, say it, say that it's a lie, that nothing... nothing happened between us..."

Tram sparks appeared in my eyes. I only saw Nana taking out a microphone from her cleavage and starting to prepare a news report. And then everything moved or, more precisely, everything moved around.

I flew out of the restaurant and started to run. The speed gave birth to rails, rails, rails, rails... My throat is burning. I won't go home. There's no getting away from the idiots--they'll break my nose and mouth again, they'll force me to sweep up the broken pieces. Rails, rails... I don't even know where I am anymore. The Square clock rang. Let me lie down under it until the dizziness goes away. My feet slipped before I could reach the clock.

The Square is running and I'm running after it. It passed by Rossya Cinema laughing out loud. Gagik's pop art face was glued by the entrance. It flew over the statue of Davit of Sasun. Gagik was sitting in front of Davit trying to move Kurkik Jalali [27] with spiky spurs. It went into the subway, left behind the rails, and rose again into the lighted world. At every station Gagik's face whizzed past me and caused my nose to bleed...

The Square ran and ran for about ten minutes and then hurled me somewhere that was very far from our house...

I remember the second Wednesday well. I woke up with boiling coffee on my tongue. I want to drink. Gagik and Edita were sitting next to the table watching TV. The woman had somehow withered and turned black from the long road. My heart fluttered when I recalled her body that was tight and slippery like a fish.

Gagik has not talked to me since that day. And Edita, thinking that she's the cause of our row, doesn't let anyone near her number.

A singing bird appeared on the screen. Gagik changed the channel irritated and got even more irritated.

They had not filmed all of the minister; only his face was visible. It was his last interview.

"Please accept our condolences..."

"Thank you..."

"I know that this is not the most appropriate time to ask, but, nevertheless, how are you feeling?"

"Better already... Though worse at the same time..."

"Has your mother ever been a symbol of the Homeland for you?"

"My mother was everything for me: my homeland, my past, my childhood..."

"How, with what methods, did your mother sow love for the homeland? Through fairy tales?"

---

27 Davit of Sasun's horse.

"I was never told fairy tales..."

I pushed my tongue that was burned by System in the coffee cup.

"How many times?"

"What?"

"I'm asking how many times you screwed Lili."

"Forget about it..."

"Were you drunk?"

"I don't remember."

"Where did you finish the job?"

"Gag..."

"What Gag? What color underwear was she wearing?"

"I don't want it..."

"You don't want it? What about Lili? Did she want it?"

Gagik's body contorted like plasticine. His voice turned off. He opened and closed his mouth a few times and attacked me. He caught my fist in the air, pulled my hair, and shoved my phone in my eye. A bitchy smell emanated from the message Lili had written. I couldn't take it anymore. I slapped him. The city *fleeted* again. Gagik and I did somersaults in the air, colliding against each other, while Edita was trying to separate us with her arms spread out. I was running and Gagik was running after me. And then he was running, kicking the windows of the cars of idiots...

The city was *fleeting*, then slowing down, stopping, photographing the captured images, and then *fleeting* again.

The door--*fleeted*... The police officer's moustache--*fleeted*... The car--*fleeted*... The police station--*fleeted*... The door of the police chief's office--*fleeted*... The chair--*fleeted*... Me on that chair--*fleeted*...

"Are we going to be silent for a long time?" The interrogator was a plump twenty-two, twenty-three year old guy.

"What do you want to talk about?"

"You mean, what do you want to talk about?"

"It's all the same to me..."

"What, the topic of discussion or your admission of the crime?"

"What crime?"

"I'm joking..."

He had a *rabis* ring and thick chain on his right hand and repulsive gold on his incisor.

"Because of you, your friend's father resorted to sui-ci..."

"Because of me?"

"No doubt about it... That's what more than ten eye-witnesses claimed they saw. Before pulling the trigger, he pointed at you and addressed you with words close to these: 'I knew it. I knew you were a bastard and that you'd disgrace me like this in the end.'"

My tongue felt excited at the wish of having charred, burned coffee. Rock attacked me.

Anna tried to get me to sing twice.

"But you have a voice, and you have good hearing, but as soon as you open your mouth, crows flock together."

"But I'm not a singer..."

"I'm not saying you're a singer... I want to sing with you."

"Anna, can't you see that it's not working?"

"Try. As you're singing, when you take a breath, let the same sensation come up in you that you feel when your tongue is burning."

The interrogator's crassness turned to humanism for a moment.

"What happened? You're not getting enough air?"

"No, everything's fine..."

"Would you like some coffee?"

"Sure."

The button turned red in my eye. The door opened--and *fleeted*. A military woman in a miniskirt--*fleeted*. The tray with the wobbling cups--*fleeted*. Slurp, I took the first sip--and *fleeted*.

"Why did they assign the minister's case to you specifically?"

"What do you mean?"

"Aren't you still too young for this?"

"Mastering the profession is what's important. Our country is young and needs young professionals."

"With the ambitions of an adult?"

"You say that the minister had no reason and that you were not the reason..."

"I don't know..."

"Were you invited?"

"No... I was looking for my friend Gagik."

"They had seen each other before you came. The son firmly shook his father's hand before he left."

"I have nothing to say. I probably can't help you."

"I know... But before he started shooting, the minister got angry with you specifically..."

My phone woke up from the *rabis* babble. I picked up.

"I'm sorry... One second... No, I can't right now. I'm busy."

Anna's smile appeared on my lips. Sometimes I want to smile like her. I don't know, I have a feeling it probably works.

"Why are you smiling?"

"No reason. I remembered something."

"Could it be that our ancestors' hair has grown?"

"What do you mean?"

"I heard your interview on the radio. They also showed it on TV a year ago, didn't they? Do you really have documents like that?"

"Like what?"

"That you're a descendant of the royal Cilicia dynasty..."

"I do..."

"I'm not saying good for you, even though my people were ordinary farmers. Instead, it seems our positions have reversed. I'm joking..."

"Good for me that you're joking..."

"Are you married?"

"No..."

"That's strange."

"What is?"

"You're the only son of your parents. Who's going to carry on your dynasty?"

"My father's..."

My nose bled from the emotions of a thirty-year-old.

"Everything is clear." He extended a tissue. "You can leave."

"Really? Goodbye... Or more precisely..."

"Don't say farewell. We'll see each other again."

"I don't understand..."

"At the second interrogation. I've already talked to Gagik. I'll talk to Anna as well and then I'll call you."

Anna's smile froze on my mouth together with my

blood.

"What does Anna have to do with this?"

"Probably nothing..."

"She..."

"Goodbye. Don't leave the city. Please."

Last Wednesday probably repeated itself five times. The calendar got stuck like a broken record.

It was ten, fifteen days ago. I had gone to a pharmacy with Gagik to buy condoms. He bought ten and gave me one. I got aroused. Instead of wonderful ideals, only a simple sexual desire and one question remained: who to fuck.

I saw Edita for the first time at the governmental reception. She didn't want to talk to me because of Lili's bitchiness.

Around seven o'clock, Anna called.

"Grig, there's a concert at the Opera at nine-thirty. Do you want to come?"

"That late?"

"It's an elite concert. I'd really like you to come."

"I'll come..."

"Don't say anything to Gagik."

"Okay, I'll say that I have to take Edita back to her hotel."

"Who's Edita?"

Anna was waiting at the main entrance.

"You're late again?" She was annoyed. "A few scum were circling around me."

Trams sparks appeared in my eyes.

"I'm sorry. You know, I feel like it's morning."

"Do church and mass exist for people like you? What did you tell Gagik?"

"Nothing..."

"Was that skank with him?"

"You mean Lili?"

"Yeah..."

"As always..."

"I remembered correctly. Who's Edita?"

What concert is it? If only they had put up an announcement or sold a program. Anna's smile froze again.

Had Gagik not been there, I would've hurt Lili. When was it that I brought her to a theater? She wanted to become an actress. And I had a friend who was a stage director. He was one of those geniuses who used needles. Lili saw him and froze--the poor girl's tongue spun in her mouth eight times before she was able to speak two-and-a-half words. Not to be rejected, he suggested for her to come and go to the theater for a while and then see. But the next day Lili was not allowed to enter the building. Her trampy mother, who thought she was saving her daughter from what she believed was a brothel, had broken the glass of the main entrance.

"Dear audience, the performance is going to begin."

The curtain fluttered open. The set on the stage looked like the interior of the minister's house, and the soloist looked exactly like him. The opera can't be about the minister, can it? I'm interested to see how they dealt with the war scenes.

The incomprehensible garble and terrible interpretation of the unknown singer's solo--oh my!--forced me to leave the venue and go to the bathroom.

I saw that Anna's seat was empty. When did she leave that I didn't notice?

Snrk... I snorted.

I have a fear of going into bathrooms. I get a feeling that there's someone in there and that that person is related to a relative or family member. Moreover, that person is most definitely a representative of the female sex.

The dressing room is on the other side of the door. I always confuse the two. One time when I wanted to go to the bathroom, I opened the door and there was a prima donna--I won't give away her name--changing her undergarments inside. The scandal she sparked! I didn't understand whether she was singing or yelling. I somehow managed to get out of that situation. The idiot demanded that I marry her.

The signs on the bathroom doors had turned upside down.

I couldn't tell which was designated for women and which for men. A man came out from the right. He was buttoning up his pants with his unwashed hands.

On the walls, there were twenty to thirty sketches of twisted "penises" and a whole bunch of profanities.

A few of the writings had a political twist. But the most political statement had been written by a sixteen-year-old youth. The content of the statement was something along these lines: "I'm ready to give myself--only to give myself--to beautiful sixteen to thirty-nine-year-old men." There was also a phone number. A few thick heterosexuals had left their profane manly announcements on the wall whose content I won't mention, because those are already more than well-known.

There were incomparably more vaginas. One of them was decked with pink lipstick.

As a kid, I was sexually aroused only twice: once in a sports field and once in a bathroom.

I was probably twelve when I saw a vagina for the first time. It was so impressive and beautiful that it made me lose my mind for two weeks. Sadly, my happiness didn't last long. A few days later the janitor of the school discovered the vagina and erased it from the bathroom wall.

Psychologically speaking, the arousal I got in the sports field was much stronger. During a game, an asshole got up and shouted as loud as he could: "Cow's penis!" For one month I asked here and there what that was and where it was. In the summer, I convinced my parents to let me go to camp. For one month I looked for a cow's penis. I didn't find it. Instead I learned how to milk cows.

The act happened suddenly, perplexingly fast and impressive.

I penetrated. Anna's naked body shivered under the shower. Her tits were hard and red, and her vagina was beautifully shaved and tailored. The water had given the delicate fuzz a light-cinnamon shade. She saw me, but didn't move--she could've at least covered whatever she could with her hands.

The water was hot. It stung the scar on my back. I ignored it and assaulted her. She didn't resist me and I could feel that she had no experience. She constantly wanted to kiss my mouth. And I was playing with her tits.

"Grig, you'll kill me..."

"No one has died of this yet."

"When you say no one, who do you mean?"

"I mean no one, eh..."

"I'll die..."

Her body was sticky like marmalade. The stickiness I felt on my fingers reminded me of the condom I had on me that Gagik had given. My heart sank for a moment.

"Do you love me," she asked.

"I do..."

"Don't lie," she said and, grabbing a clump of my hair in her fist, smashed my head against the wall.

"Are you nuts?"

"You don't love me. If you loved me you'd be with me without that."

I pressed her hips and penetrated. I heard a squeak. A gush of blood rolled down to my knee and left rusty marks on the white of the bathroom.

"I told you, didn't I, that you'd kill me?"

My phone roared. Tram sparks appeared in my eyes when I saw Gagik's number. He had sent a text.

"I love you, love you, want you..."

"Who is it?" She twitched as she rubbed her crack.

"Your brother..."

The water stopped suddenly. Clothes flew up, wrapped themselves around Anna, and hurled her out of the dressing room.

The soloist was laughing with his mouth wide open. Now go and listen to an elite concert after all this.

How do I reply to this idiot?

"Gagik, have you lost your mind? You love me and want me? Go home and sleep. Grig"

I went out... The minister was standing in front of the theater's main entrance.

The hallway that stretches to the psychologist is endless...

Saving the minister was successful. When the gun went off, his wife managed to avert the direction of the gun with a strike. He hurt his shoulder. He didn't even fall. That same day, at two in the morning, his mother, who lived in one of the border villages, passed away.

I had no choice but to go the funeral. I wanted to see Anna. Gagik's face reeked. I walked up to him to offer my condolences. Anna leaned against my shoulder sobbing and whispered:

"I don't know what to do. It's been a few days that the bleeding hasn't stopped."

"Have you gone to the doctor's?"

"Are you crazy?"

"We'll go together tomorrow."

"You want them to arrest my father?"

"What does your father have to do with this?"

"He found out about us. He beat me so much with a broom that... And in the city there are rumors that you're with my mother."

"Your father is the guilty one... I don't know. Should I go up to him and express my condolences?"

"Stay away. He's giving an interview."

"What interview?"

"About his mother and homeland... Who did you come with?"

"Edita."

"Who the hell is Edita?"

The house was rocking. The tongues that stuck out of the windows scattered cups and plates all over the court-yard. The picture of Gagik's one-hundred-year-old dead uncle appeared for a moment on one of the pockmarked glasses.

It was probably because of the palpitations of the house that they put Grandma's body in the courtyard. Her braids had spilled out of the coffin and in her hands she held a strange instrument that bore a resemblance to a welding device.

Snrk... I snorted.

Rock's heavy metal is unbearable when it's cold. I don't want to admit that death scares the crap out of me and that ghosts do, too...

It was dark in the hallway. Only one section of the apartment was visible through the open door. I went to their house once. They're Nana's kin.

The immortal great-grandmother was lying on the rotten bed with her back to me. The old aunt was standing in front of a mirror in her bra putting Chinese make-up on her face. Her stupid daughter was taking pictures of her mother in that state.

Tram sparks appeared in my eyes. I don't know where the dead Grandma came from. There was a welding device in her hand. The windows closed in the blink of an eye and the smell of menstruation in the house became unbearable. A gale and snowstorm started in the living room. The grandmother undid her braids and:

"Bless you, my dear... Get your hair cut. You're not a girl..."

She turned on the device and started to weld the footprints I had left on the snow. Fire and snow had mixed together in the room and were eating each other. The aunt was shivering and looking for her fur coat, and the immortal great-grandmother was sitting on the lid of the coffin cleaning up the snow.

Grandma's hair was spreading out and tying knots with the walls of the house. Shreds of the shed fur coat played in the air. As for the daughter... click after click after click... she was photographing all of this...

The grandmother with her hair down--*fleeted*. The

aunt with her naked body wrapped in shreds of fur coat--*fleeted*. The daughter, shaving her moustache and beard--*fleeted*. The door--*fleeted*. My hand on that door--*fleeted*.

Amiryan Street was on the threshold.

Everything started with this street. This is why no matter which direction Yerevan *fleets* in, in the end it always ends up at the crossroads of Amiryan and Zakyan.

There is a feeling of aimlessness in the summer. It's probably been a month already that the three of us go...

Edita had asked to be taken to "Heaven's Door." She was saying that it was definitely in Armenia. And, like an idiot, I promised to take her to Heaven safely.

The day starts in a hurry and ends on the other side of the sun. It's always the three of us... We're always going...

When I told the psychologist about this, he laughed.

"Do you use drugs?"

I wasn't going to say "yes," was I?

"No..."

"Does the state of Yerevan *fleeting* worry you?"

"No..."

"Then enjoy these peculiarities of the city. Especially since there's probably no other like it anywhere else."

Edita called at 11:15. We had agreed to meet at half past under the Square clock.

"I'm talking to my sister in Germany..."

"When will you come?"

"I can't come. My mother is coming back from Frankfurt." I hung up the phone and was surprised. Edita's Armenian pierced my ear for the first time. When did she learn it? What language were we communicating in all this time?

The door of my house had reached Amiryan Street at

half past. I opened the door and went out. I didn't want to see them. I couldn't do it. It's really hard to get away from Gagik. Wherever I go, I run into him. It was only yesterday that I left the house to go up to Avan, but the city didn't move an inch from Abovian Street.

"The investigator was asking about you." He didn't look my way.

"I know... He called..."

"And, so, I still don't understand why Edita's voice echoes..."

"I know what you think of me, but I hardly have anything to do with any of this."

"Anna was also called in for interrogation."

"Gag, I have something to tell you."

"I really don't care anymore. Did you also sleep with my stepmother?"

"Are you crazy?"

"I finished drawing my cartoon."

"When can we watch it?"

"There's nothing to watch..."

There was... The woman was sitting on Amiryan Street under the library wall. She had a wretched, burned face and was wearing ragged black clothes. Her head was wrapped in a kerchief. It was probably that tattered cloth that made her look twenty years her age. Her legs were spread out and shameless. Her corruption shrieked from her wounds. They were big dark-red specks, as if her body had been dunked in raspberry jam.

The empty "Poison" bottle pressed in the palm of her hand gave birth to sun bunnies. It smelled like smoked fish. I don't know why it seemed like the smell was blowing from the crumpled-up wet paper on which the woman had sprawled and was not moving.

Gagik was fumbling his pockets.

"What are you looking for?"

"Royal son, give me a bit of money."

The heavy metal rang. My finger got stuck on a fifty-dram coin and wouldn't let go. I pulled off my finger with it and tossed the money to the woman.

. The woman raised her head and looked at Edita with surprise. Her eyes widened and her question resounded like the sound of an electric guitar:

"You got married to the one with the long hair?"

For a moment, Edita did not understand her question. About a minute was required for the fisher's wife's face to reinstate itself in her brain. She didn't know what to say and whatever she said would sound fake. The shining eyes of the "Poison" were piercing. Without saying a word, Edita moved closer to hug the woman, but Yerevan caught her by the nape with Zakyan's hook and hurled her to the airport.

The announcer's stuffy nose made her sound like Armenian pop music. The lava of rock was powerless here. Shitty "music" devours everything, including heavy metal.

The tram sparks burned my eyes. For about five minutes, the fireworks wouldn't slack off.

That light...

Light can also be ailing. It makes you both sleepy and sleepless. It awakens masochistic thrills.

The light at the airport has darkness in it. This is probably why departing people resemble shadow plays. There are black sketches on a white human-sized *rabis* contrivance. Each time people come and go behind it, it rings. The ring probably says goodbye to Yerevan.

"Every time I go abroad I get a strange feeling. It's as if I'll find myself in Heaven if I pass through security," Edita played with Armenian words with love.

"Don't worry about it. We'll find Heaven's Door..."

A real face appeared in the shadow play. It was Vahagn. He chewed on cigarette butts when he couldn't smoke weed.

He saw us and... He was grinding his teeth--this was probably his way of trying to hide Armenia's sorrow in him.

"Grig, thank you, really thank you... You're the only one who came to see me off..."

Gagik was in Vahagn's yellow eyes looking like he was firing in a shooting range. He couldn't take it in the end and kissed him hard on the mouth.

"Gag, my friend, I'm also gratefully to you. I did good to many people, but on this day no one came to say goodbye to me except for you two..."

"Where are you flying to?"

My question drove the city mad. Vahagn didn't get a chance to open his mouth. Yerevan slapped Zvartnots [28] to provide those departing from the country with favorable conditions. By the time the idiot came to, the airplanes had flown up and vanished like sparks.

Vahagn's words became ethereal.

"Go to our house every now and again and water the flowers."

The teeth of the keys sawed my finger.

The city welcomed my mother with open arms.

Gagik's car moved with the pace of a turtle.

---

28 Zvartnots is Armenia's main international airport.

"Drive faster..."

"You've told me to slow down until now..."

"No, it's fine." It's my mother. "I'm the one who asked you to drive slowly. I've missed Yerevan..."

Because my mother had missed Yerevan, it took us two hours to get home instead of fifteen or twenty minutes. Gagik left the car out. Our gate is narrow like the throat of a whale.

The smell of pop music emanated from the house.

"How many days have you not been home?" With a microscope in her hand, my mother was trying to discover traces of the deeds I had done in three weeks.

"I don't remember. Probably two..."

"Gagik, how many days has my son not slept at home?"

"No idea," Gagik's face immediately turned into pop art. "Name it, we went there. In the end, we ended up in the village..."

"I heard... I'm sorry."

"Thanks... How's your daughter?"

"She's fine. They're getting a house in the next two months. They'll move out of the camp. Well, aren't you coming in?"

"Let's go in..."

"Grigor, you could've at least left the window open... What is this smell?"

"No idea... I left the radio on. As usual, they're playing the songs of our pop stars."

Rock music flooded from my mother's screams. The words "Ne dazhdyoshsya menya, petlya" on the wall of my room turned upside down.

"Mom, what happened?"

"Come and see for yourself..."

That day my cat had woken up by itself. It had gone into my room and had not found me there. Every morning the scoundrel would come and sit on my head forever until I woke up. I hit it once or twice, but it still didn't get it.

It probably cursed me in its head and went back to sleep in the heat. It had woken up, mewed, hopped on my bed, and gone out into the garden. It had seen its filled bowl of food, but had not eaten it. It had probably not been hungry. It had come back inside the house, had stared and stared at the John Lennon photograph on the dresser and had missed me.

That night it had slept in my bed, hugging my pillow.

It had woken up in the morning and probably gone crazy when it didn't find me. Like someone who's lost his mind, it had jumped up and tilted the glass frame around John Lennon's photograph. And then, hungry and thirsty, it had scratched my jeans, hugged my slippers to inhale my scent, and waited all day.

My cat had died with its mouth open, without mewing. The expression on its face, like that of a person dying alone, was wild. In its sharp and savage claws, there was something gentle about the way they held my slippers...

The hallway, fuck you...

I opened the door and went it. There was a banquet. The minister's wife, who was standing by the door, ordered the bodyguard to let me in with a doe-like hand gesture. Again? It's repeating again?

Anna was screaming or, more precisely, she was urging me to sing some sort of unknown duet with incomprehensible words.

"But you have a voice, and you have good hearing, but as soon as you open your mouth, crows flock together."

"But I'm not a singer..."

"I'm not saying you're a singer... I want to sing with you."

"Anna, can't you see that it's not working?"

"Try. As you're singing, when you take a breath, let the same sensation come up in you that you feel when your tongue is burning."

"Has your bleeding stopped?"

"Yeah... Did you get really scared?"

"Was I not supposed to? You're sixteen."

"Eighteen..."

"Gagik was saying that..."

"I'm eighteen. It's been two years now that I don't exist to Gagik, that I'm as old to him as I was before. Did your tongue burn?"

She's holding onto my wrist and forcing me to sing the high notes. I'm screaming way and way out of tune. Suddenly I turned around and what do I see? The hall is filled to the brim. The audience is clapping, prompting the lyrics of the song, spitting, and throwing rotten eggs. What can I do? Suddenly the head of the former fisher, Valodik, popped out from under the stage. He opened up the latest Playboy issue, colored one of the girl's nipples dark, looked into my eyes, and, picking his nose, asked:

"Are you coming on Wednesday?"

"What?"

"Grig," Anna pulled my arm, "he's prompting your text. Repeat it."

"Are you coming on Wednesday?" I repeated with a voice close to rock.

"I don't know," the prima donna Anna was in her element.

Valodik shook his head. I understood. He had moved on to painting other parts.

"It's already the third Wednesday that you haven't come."

I repeated the words.

"Do you see that door? That artificial, decorative door? Open it and enter the stage." Anna's operatic voice scratched my rock-accustomed ears.

"But we're already on stage."

"The mise en scène is like that. Grig, hurry up..."

I ran, opened the door, and...

It's hard to tell why I had a wet dream.

"What happened?" Edita's wizened body had become gentle, tight, and smooth.

"I had a bad dream..."

"You fell asleep with your eyes closed?"

"No, for a moment I had a theatrical nightmare." My wet trousers were sticking to my thigh.

"I see... What building is this?"

"It's the Dramatic Theater. One day, when it's a good time, we'll come watch a performance."

"For you to have nightmares again?"

"Where's Gagik?"

"You can't take a step without Gagik?"

"I don't know... Aren't we going?"

"Where?"

"The place you said. Let's keep going until we get to Heaven's Door."

"I remember a movie. The heroes keep going and going. They each dream about each other. And then they would go again, just like us... Only the heat was missing."

"Are you tired?"

"No…"

"Do you want to go for a run?"

The day changed--and *fleeted*… The night lights turned on--and *fleeted*… The cafe emptied--and *fleeted*… Valodik appeared at our table--and *fleeted*…

"Good morning!" A *rabis* smell blew out of the boy's mouth.

"Hi…"

"Hey man, do you have a second?"

The cafe's Coca-Cola redness cast a shadow over Edita.

"What is it?"

"I have a really cool porn mag… Wanna buy it?"

"Let me see it."

Snrk… I snorted…

A butt was lying on a bed wearing granny panties. The page had got stuck to my finger and wouldn't turn. I licked it… The wetness of my pants made itself felt again.

"You look and I'll be back soon…"

On the blouse was the old aunt with her tissue paper breasts. There were a few crazy poses: wearing a bra, standing naked in front of a mirror with thousand-year-old feathers thrown over her shoulders.

The Chinese patterns weighed more. The old aunt was filling tea in a rusty cup with the grace of an Armenianized geisha.

It was like a sexual monarchy. The great-grandmother's picture was only in one place. Their bashful daughter didn't even appear. Her only chore in the household business was probably to take pictures. Fuck you… Why am I surprised? Aren't they Nana's kith and kin?

In the end there were also a few surrealist photographs. The aunt, wearing sunglasses, welding the door of the house, and do you really want me to tell you how big the great-grandmother's butt was compared to the light bulb she was changing? The last photograph, serving to sum all of this up: the aunt, with her breasts veiled under black tulle, standing by the lid of the coffin.

Tram sparks appeared in my eyes.

The grandmother's ghost whirred in my head once more.

The red and the white on the black of the photographs were melding and eating each other up. And suddenly the pictures started to make noise.

"You son of a bitch, what the fuck are you doing?"

The bellowing of the bull blew up the aunt's bra.

A few assholes pulled my hair, twisted my arms, and scraped my face against the ground...

Yerevan suddenly turned into a desert. The theater, Nairi Cinema, and Moskovyan Park held Edita in their arms and made it to Paris in one second. The redness of Coca-Cola stayed behind and I was face-to-face with the idiots.

"So, you're now pissing in public places, eh?"

"Who?" The power of rock hardened my insides.

"That shitface..."

"Valodik?"

"Very good... And then you ask, 'who?'..."

"Let go of my hands..."

"Let go. He won't run... What magazine is this?" The chief bull took the magazine and started to flick through it. "Oh my... Turns out you're a proper degenerate. It's not good, not good..."

"Give the magazine back to its owner. Goodbye..."

"Wait a second..."

"Yes." The heavy metal won't let me break.

"You piss in our brother's restaurant and say goodbye, eh? So," the bull's bellow made my nose bleed, "you think you're a good guy, don't you? You have to clean up your piss."

"What?" The coffee burned my tongue again.

"Somebody, bring a broom!"

A commotion broke out that only ended when the broom appeared. They brought the broom solemnly, upholding all the subtleties of a ritual. I felt the taste of repetition again.

"Sweep, I say." I couldn't see the bull and his voice caused a short circuit in my ears. "He wants you to piss blood. Either way you'll have to clean it up. Or do you not know who we are?"

"I won't clean it up..."

The shitty words and clusters of sounds from Armenian pop music devoured the heavy metal.

"Argh," the bull was scratching his balls, "I love this chick so much... She sings well, doesn't she, Blondie... Did you fuck her good? Wipe your nose... Those sissies, you don't even touch them and they break."

"You're the sissy..."

"Eh... Blondie, wait. No, you misunderstood. That wasn't about you. Hey, don't you want to go home? Your mom made all these nice little meals. You'll eat them and grow stronger... Huh? Just tell me where Valodik is..."

"I don't know..."

"I said..."

"I said I don't know..."

"Blondie, did you see that? A new Pavlik Morozov [29] has appeared... Fine, bro. But as far as I remember, that Pavlik didn't have long hair, did he, Blondie? Sure thing. Should we not shave his hair, so he understands who's who in this city..."

The scissors flew up and fell into the bull's hand.

"Stop flapping around. You're not a chicken..."

They cut my hair and snuffed out the fire of rock with the sewage of pop music.

"Having long hair for me is nothing to be ashamed of, man. We're moving toward Europe, we're doing things... What's important to me is to mess you up so bad that your own mother doesn't recognize you. What is that, you standing there giving interviews saying that you're the king of Armenians? You know now, right, who the owner of this country is?"

"It's not you, is it?"

"Don't worry, you'll know... Tomorrow or the day after when they take away the ground from under your house and build a casino in its place, you'll know... You'll know..."

My cut hair itched. The itch flapped in my throat. I flapped until the scissors fell out of the bull's hand. The half-blunt blade tore the redness of Coca-Cola and hurled me home.

For about ten minutes, the throat of the whale did not let me in.

My mother was standing behind the window waiting. Her eyes widened in surprised so much that the windows shattered into pieces.

"What happened to you?"

---

29 Pavlik Morozov (1918-1932) denounced his father and was killed soon after by his family. He was considered a martyr in the Soviet Union.

"Thank God..."

"Why are you thanking God?"

"Nothing... I'm mourning for my cat."

"I got that," my mother started to sweep the shards of glass. "But why did you mess up your head?"

"Do you recognize me?"

"I don't understand..."

"I was afraid you wouldn't recognize me..."

"You're crazy." My mother held the broom like an electric guitar and sang a line from Nirvana, "How can I not recognize my own blood?"

"It's so hot... What did you do to the cat, mom?"

"I buried it under the tree... Grig, you haven't forgotten, have you? It's your father's tenth anniversary on Wednesday."

I tightened the spring in my head to stop the ghosts from roaming around. My nose bled.

"I haven't forgotten."

"You're bleeding again?"

"I'm tired." I felt that I missed rock's heavy metal and immediately felt a thirst for coffee.

"If you're tired, get married... We'll live, eh, a house, a place... That reminds me. Grig, two big shots came yesterday and said that our house and property are not in our name. I told them a million times to check the cadaster and sort everything there..."

"What do you mean?"

"Just like that." My mother cut her finger sweeping the glass with a wet cloth. The smell of rust hit my nose and I involuntarily heard the bellow of the bull. "Everything is possible in this country... Is this life? It's been ten years and we still can't lay a stone over your father's grave..."

My inner spring couldn't take it. The lava of rock spilled over so suddenly that I didn't manage to say "Mom, I love you very much..."

The hallway that stretches to the psychologist is endless...

Two people were standing there arguing. One of them was Valodik with a bundle of porn magazines under his arm.

"It's already the second he's coming..."

Passages appeared in his eyes as he talked. I walked up to say a few words about the piss when an unbearable gale and snowstorm started.

"Are you coming on Wednesday?" Valodik changed the topic when he saw me.

"I don't know," the face of the speaker was not visible.

"You can't do that. It's the third Wednesday you haven't come..."

The minister lying in the coffin in our living room has taken my father's smile on his face. They're constantly killing this poor man. What wrong he has done, I don't know.

There was a welding device between his fingers, which were like my father's fingers. Nana's old aunt was standing at the head of the deceased with her breasts covered in black tulle. What about that immortal great-grandmother? She was standing with her behind to me farting constantly.

The idiots also appeared. When she heard their bellows, the aunt turned coquettish. But the bulls paid no attention to her. In their eyes was Nana dancing in her red dress.

The chief bull locked eyes with me, scratched his balls, and bellowed:

"Have you asked your lover where we meet every Wednesday?"

"What lover?"

"The one who will break her promise the day after tomorrow..."

"How did this dead person appear in our house?"

"You don't know? It's all legal... I told you, didn't I, that we'll take your house from you and turn it into a funeral parlor? I told you, didn't I?"

"I won't clean it..."

"What? Dude, this guy has totally lost his mind. As soon as we corner him a bit and yell at him, he remembers the broom... Somebody, bring the broom. Let him sweep..."

I flew out and started to run. The speed gave birth to rails, rails, rails, rails... My throat is burning. I won't go home. There's no getting away from the bulls--is that even a question? Is it my house or? Rails, rails... My eyes are getting moist... Again I don't recognize Yerevan. The Square clock rang. Let me lie down under it until the dizziness goes away. Again? My feet slipped before I could reach the clock.

The Square was running and I was running after it. It cackled past First District. Instead of a worker, the statue of one of the bulls had been erected with Gagik's pop art face on his chest. It ran over the mouth of the gorge until Hrazdan and then suddenly appeared in Zeytun, tore up the posters that were hung on walls with the heads of bulls on them, and flew on top of Tamanyan's--the statue's--back. [30]

After running for about ten minutes, the city hurled me out of the city...

I was out of the city for three days.

I snorted and the sun set... I snorted and it rose... That huge, burning sphere gave and took summer from the earth.

The sun devoured the earth, spat it out, then swallowed it again, and threw it up again...

For three days the city did not let me in. Finally it caught me by the neck with Raykom's hook and hurled me into the police station.

"I had asked you," the investigator's plumpness had deflated and he had turned a little yellow, "I had asked you, no, not to leave the city?"

"You had..."

"What, did I have to give you an order for you to obey? It's been three days that I've been looking for you..."

"It was against my will... I couldn't come back to Yerevan..."

"You didn't have any money?"

"No, there were other issues."

A brotherly smile appeared on the investigator's face.

"It's not your health, is it?"

"Thank God, I have nothing to complain about..."

"So it's about a girl. I'm sorry. I try not to think about the private life of the one sitting across from me..."

"And what if your work requires it?"

"That's different... I spoke with Anna..."

"And?" A desire to pull on the investigator's cheeks

---

30 Alexander Tamanyan (1878-1936) was an architect who built the central plan of Yerevan city. His statue stands in central Yerevan.

arose in me. I imagined him playing with a teddy bear as a child. I'm sure he didn't have anything like Legos and stuff. At the very, very most he might have had like a ten or fifteen-centimeter dump truck to move twigs as small as his pinkie and a handful of sand from one end of the table to the next...

"And? For how many years have your known Gagik?"

"I don't know... Probably two..."

"It's amazing. You're a grown-up man, but you're friends with a twenty-one-year-old boy."

"There are boys of twenty-two who run legal cases for ministers."

"Am I to take your words as a compliment, Grigor?"

"Grigor? You probably mean 'sir'..."

"I'm sorry, sir, you're right..."

I only just then noticed that the *rabis* ring and chain had disappeared.

"And you, are you married?"

"Divorced... But that has no bearing whatsoever on the case. Anna was very scared."

"Why?"

"Well... She was scared that your relationship would be known to many people."

"What relationship?"

The investigator's cheeks puffed out and plumped up.

"Whatever the case may be, you were in a relationship at some point."

"What draws you to that conclusion?"

"We were taught to read facial features for five years straight. And you know why? To not believe the words of the likes of you..."

"The likes of me? Don't tell me they also gave Princess Diana's case to you. Speaking of which, what is your name, Mister Investigator?"

"Citizen Gasparyan... In short, it's because of you that..."

"Because of me? Did I shoot? Did I put the gun in the minister's hand? Did anyone of those present hear a single bad word come out of my mouth? He's the one who insulted me, calling me an 'asshole'..."

Investigator Gasparyan stretched out. His tension made the inkwell and cigarette pack run from one end of the table to the next just like the toy dump truck.

"Okay... Why are you friends with someone eleven years younger? You don't belong to the same class... So what if one of your ancestors was the illegitimate son of some Francophile king. You don't work. They say you live off your generous sister who lives in a German refugee camp... Day after day you're with Gagik and now you're getting Anna..."

"Don't involve Anna in this case..."

"Have you talked to Gagik?"

"About what?"

"Well... How do Armenian men do this? Before starting a romantic relationship, they first have to introduce themselves to the girl's brother, talk to him, come to an agreement, and only then..."

"And only then go to a sauna or motel..."

"Did you go to a sauna?"

"And you were saying that you try not to think about other people's private lives..."

"If the case doesn't require it..."

The unemployed inkwell ran over one of the investigator's pens.

"Are there any other questions?"

"There are... Why did you clash with Gagik?"

"That's irrelevant to the case."

"What about the minister's wife?"

"Citizen Gasparyan, you made a mistake in choosing your profession. You should work for the International League of Sexual Reforms."

"With pleasure, only on one condition, however, that you become my chief advisor on deviant sexuality."

"Can I go?"

"On the condition that you leave a note stating that you will not leave the city."

Condition upon condition upon condition...

The cigarette pack tipped over. The smokes spilled out and one of them appeared between the investigator's lips.

"I can't give you a note... It's been days--probably ten days now--that Yerevan is *fleeting*. I don't want to leave the city, but the city is forcing me out. For three days it wouldn't let me in. You never know where or on what street you'll end up. We're in Raykom now, right? If I left the building now, I don't know, I'll probably be in Charbakh or Shengavit..."

The smoke burned--and *fleeted*... My fingers pinched the investigator's cheeks--and *fleeted*... The shutter circled three times around the military woman standing by the door--and *fleeted*... My words stayed behind unglued--and *fleeted*... Yerevan took me to the zoo--and *fleeted*...

The third or fourth Wednesday was like a Sunday.

It wasn't dark in the hallway. I walked and...

"One cup of Parisian coffee, only boil it well, please..."

Until the barman at Artbridge[31] put rock on the fire, I snorted in my head...

The funeral procession slid behind the Urartian windows. I saw Anna among the keeners... She looked terrible. There was a kind of shameless sadness in her gaze. I don't know why my stomach churned. I wanted to love her for a minute. It's probably from not loving... I extended my hand to hold on to her hair, but the Grandmother appeared from an unknown place and whirred in my head. She was holding a welding device in her hand like a gun and roaring:

"Take good care of that child!"

Instead I petted her hair the way I petted my cat back in the day.

"You're late again?" Anna complained, probably feeling that I'm not caressing her. "A few scum were circling around me."

"Whose funeral is it?"

"My father's..."

"He died? Of what?"

"A mine..."

"But the war ended a long time ago."

"It still needs to get started." Anna was sobbing with the ambition of a proper prima donna. "The President posthumously awarded my father with the medal 'For Courage'..."

"Where's Gagik?"

"Don't know... Are you dallying with him all day? Who are you waiting for?"

Who are you waiting for? What's it to you? John Doe. All of you women collectively, I don't know what you want

<hr>

31 Artbridge is a bookstore cafe on Abovian Street.

from me. You, that bitch Lili...

It's not the time to walk out on Anna, but...

"I'm waiting for Edita..."

"You're killing us with that Edita... Who is she, eh?"

Snrk... I snorted.

The air of the zoo was suffused with sadism. The bitterness of the cages has always oppressed me. I didn't like going to the zoo even as a child--they neither let you feed the animals, nor do they feed them.

"You need permission to see it," the worker in a white coat was shelling sunflower seeds with one hand and scratching her armpit with the other.

"Why? Is it a rare beast?"

"Yes, it's a beast."

She smelled the scent of money faster than I could take it out of my pocket.

"Fine, let me take you, but fast..."

"I understand... Can the beast run away?"

"No, by letting you I could get reprimanded..."

An encaged hallway or, more precisely, a hallway of cages.

"This is the beast you wanted to see..."

I moved closer... In the cage, in a gray polka-dot nightgown, Anna's mother was looking at me with doe eyes. She looked like a statue, but her being a statue didn't last long. She jumped up and... she rammed her hoof hands through the cage and grabbed my throat.

"Well say it, say it's all a lie, that nothing happened between... that nothing happened between us... Why did you give my husband horns? Why? Asshole, Grig, I hate you..."

Tram sparks appeared in my eyes. My stupid head for

coming to the zoo. I kicked her hooves. The orderlies jumped on me, but instead of calming down the crazy woman, they put me in a strait jacket.

The doe woman froze--and *fleeted*. A drop of water squirted out of the syringe--and *fleeted*. They pulled down my jeans--and *fleeted*. The doctor's goat chin appeared through the bars--and *fleeted*.

"It's nothing," the voice was that of the closed airport, "he abused the drug a little... That's why he's talking nonsense and saying things like the city not letting him in for three days or that it regularly *fleets*... Don't worry, he'll get well, he won't die..."

August was not moving.

Edita was sitting across from me, her legs spread and whiter than white.

"They let you out of the insane asylum?" I brought the doe woman to mind somehow.

"What insane asylum?" Edita got up to bring ice coffee. "Are you seeing nightmares again?"

"Where are we now?"

"In Ararat..."

"Already?"

"We're still in the hotel... They say heaven is on Ararat, right?"

The heat was rolling down drop by drop.

"What are you looking for?"

"I lost my brush..."

"Again?"

The matter happened suddenly perplexingly fast and impressive.

Edita's body--tight, slippery, wet... She stroked my tongue with her tongue. I kissed her deep and long, not letting her breathe.

"You're killing me... How much you like to kiss!" She said and tore open the buttons of my jeans. "You're not wearing anything under it?"

"I am..."

"It's thick..."

"You wanted it to get thinner in ten days? I told you, no? Don't worry, no one has died of it yet..."

The butterflies swarmed in the air. Edita caught one of them and...

"Where did you get that from?"

"I stole it from Gagik..."

"Where's Gagik?"

"You can't stand being without him, can you?"

I penetrated without sparing anything. My body inside Edita's body was spinning in the room. I didn't destroy anything, did I? There wasn't a thing that I didn't tip over. The watermelon on the table fell and painted Edita's nipples red.

"I like watermelon a lot," she said and started to lick my body...

Red streams were squirting out of my mouth. She tore apart the watermelon, brought her mouth to my mouth, nibbled on my lips, and sucked out the juice.

The sun was going down and the watermelon was turning over--we were inside each other... It would rise and turn over--we were inside each other...

The huge, burning globe, giving and taking heat to the earth, was rubbing the juice of summer on our bodies...

Dawn broke three days later when Edita was not in bed...

The day was probably Wednesday. I got up. There was a package with papers on the table. I picked it up. My mouth froze and all the tram sparks in the folder suddenly appeared in my eyes...

"Edita, thank you for agreeing to do this interview."

"I don't do interviews, but when you suggested that I talk about your country, I felt a sort of sad worry... And then, to decline someone twice on the same matter seemed wrong to me. It's just that it's a little difficult to do an interview when you're swimming in the Sevan..."

"Edita, what is happiness for you?"

"You always ask the same questions. Happiness is when you feel good and that, believe me, happens very rarely. Generally I don't feel anything or I feel time slowing down, which, as it becomes clear later, turns out that it went by five times faster in fast-forward..."

"And, Edita, what do you do to be happy?"

"I try not to think about getting old."

"It's been a month that you have been in Armenia. What are your impressions of our country?"

"I agreed to come to Armenia, because my grandmother was always saying that the door that leads to Heaven is in your country... I would very much like to see that door."

"Are you scared of death?"

"No... Finding Heaven's Door doesn't mean to die."

"There's an age-old conflict between Armenians and..."

"Yes, I am a Turk. I feel that conflict. I don't think it will disappear in the next fifty years..."

"And how do you feel about the Genocide?"

"I can't believe it. A hundred years haven't even

passed yet, but I still can't believe that something like that is possible..."

"Do you accept the evidence?"

"What do you want me to say? Today is interested in being today. The fingers on your hands are not the same, are they? I think we can consider the case closed."

"Can you talk about your first love?"

"I can say one thing: that I had different feelings every time I made love to him. The first time I hated it, and then I truly loved it, and then I was disgusted by it, and then I would go crazy. I think love is like that. Every time you get intimate, you feel different things..."

"Is that why you are afraid to love?"

"Probably..."

"And do you have any Armenian friends?"

"I do... Both of them are guys... A few days ago, my friend Grigor was taken to an insane asylum."

"Why?"

"For not approaching questions in a standard fashion. He had said something or other to the investigator about the city, about which they are normally quiet, and he had decided to send Grigor to an asylum."

"And?"

"I was forced to say that Grigor was a Turkish citizen."

"Are going to stay long in Yerevan?"

"I don't know... In any case, I've already found 'Heaven's Door'... I've even come close to the door once..."

"Really? Where is it?"

Should I say it was out of horror, out of stupidity, or out of I don't know what that I ate the papers. There was a whole printing-house of letters in my throat.

Flee... Flee...

To flee from the city so fast that even if it ran for ten years it wouldn't catch up with me.

To get away, to erase from my brain the letters, the summer, and also Yerevan...

I shoved my finger down my throat, puked up Edita's thoughts, and opened the door. Gagik was at the door. The shutter spun him around a couple of times and threw him on the bed. I stretched my hand out by about two meters, put it in Gagik's pocket, and pulled out the bunch of keys and condoms...

The car swallowed me... Home? I'm going home? I pushed the pedal down so hard that the car played jazz. It devoured Avan in the blink of an eye and came out near Tsitsernakaberd.

I pushed down with all my strength. The wheels twitched from the screech. Have I missed my ho... home? The car melted away Komitas and came out near Tsitsernakaberd again... I couldn't take it. Irritated, I made it screech again. The monument of the Great Tragedy [32] appeared again...

The globe of the sun rolled--I was close to Ararat's peak. The moon split in half, and I was standing in front of the thin thread-like fire. When the earth gave birth to the sun, I was there again...

Wherever Yerevan *fleets*, in the end it ends up at Tsitsernakaberd.

For a moment, the Grandmother's ghost whirred in my head. Edita licked the red of the watermelon and asked:

"What is there over there?"

The grandmother made the welding device "bang

---

32 The Armenian Genocide.

bang" like a gun and roared out:

"Don't worry, it's the Turks..."

And she started to mix fire and snow...

Snrk...

Without snorting, my pupils split in half. I saw all of Yerevan's streets at the same time...

The *fleeting* city was visible to me in its entirety...

Gagik had not shown up at Vahagn's house by chance.

This was a Wednesday and I was out of town. That's why I had asked Gagik to come and water the flowers.

The teeth of the keys had pierced Gagik's finger. He had opened the door, put his finger in his mouth, and sucked up the blood.

The smell of the house had reminded Gagik of his mother. He had gone to open the window when he saw his picture in a corner in front of the computer. He had taken the photograph, had held it under the light, and had drawn traces of lips on it. A cartoon had taken over his head. Vahagn's tongue had jumped out of the cartoon, pushed the keys of the computer, and turned it on. On the screen was Gagik's picture. The tongue had played around again, opening files. The lungs of the computer, filled with gay porn photography, had exhaled and Gagik's eyes had been filled with men screwing each other. And then it had exhaled again, opened up e-mails, and had forced him to relive familiar words.

The greatest invention after the "Theory of Relativity" has been virtual reality. The internet is a mix of fairy tale and reality--a thing that you would neither consider a fairy tale, because it is a fairy tale, nor call reality, because it is reality.

"There was a guy whose virtual name was Grigor. He

wrote a ten-page letter, which he ended with words to this effect: 'I hand over my letter to the internet's ocean and wait for your reply, even if you do not exist.'"

I replied. I probably wanted to prove my existence. He wrote again, asking to meet him in a chat room. And then it started. Every day, after ten o'clock, we would meet and chat.

A week later another guy showed up in the chat room who knew everything about me: where I go, what I do, what I wear even. I thought Grigor had told him everything, but some time later the guy confessed that he was in fact Grigor. He said that he was born in Armenia and that he lived there, even though he hates his country, that in the last two months he has been following me, and that I know him, but of course not as Grigor. Turns out he's gay. He likes me and he thanks fate that he was at least able to express his love virtually.

There was also a final e-mail. It was addressed to him and that's why he read it.

"Dear Gagik, I won't send this letter, that's why I'm writing it. It's impossible to live in this city. I'm going to Holland. Everyone thinks I chose Holland to smoke weed, but you found out, right, what the real reason is? I'm only scared of one thing, of forgetting you. You remember one time you said that Yerevan is *fleeting?* I'm packing my clothes and begging the city: dear Yerevan, *fleet* in such a way so that I get to see Gagik one last time...

Take care... Love you, Vahagn..."

The *fleeting* city was visible to me in its entirety...

They looked for the drowned fisher for two days before finding him. They were saying that it was the curse of the Sevan Dragon--in the last year, the fisher had caught

1516 fish--and that's why the carriage that collapsed on the day of the funeral caused the deaths of three people.

Valodik couldn't wait for the seven days to pass, [33] so he brought his dad's car back to life and fled to the city.

After burying the dead one way or another, the fisher's wife also disappeared.

With a vodka bottle full of raspberry jam in her hand, she was running, burning in shame and pain. But she barely made it to Yerevan's threshold when the city slipped and broke the vodka bottle.

The fisher's wife's legs were painted in big red specks from top to bottom.

They say that strange characters appear in the former carriage at night. It's probably Sevan's Dragon with her hair down, wailing like Anush, looking for her dead lover. [34]

She walked around for two days hungry and thirsty, and in the end she sat down under the wall of the library and started to beg. A few bulls proposed a "good" job, but she declined.

The library wall somehow inspired a feeling of intelligence. The woman was convinced that she would find her son right there. After all, hadn't Valodik come to Yerevan to study at the institute?

The boy saw his mother once, but did not go up to her. The red specks on her legs had looked like signs of prostitution from a distance.

---

33 In Christian Armenian tradition, the bereaved remember the departed on the seventh and fortieth day after their death.

34 "Anush" (1890-1902) is a narrative poem by Hovhannes Tumanyan. In the poem, Anush's brother and husband engage in a friendly spar, but instead of letting her brother win, Anush's husband beats her brother, thereby breaking an age-old custom and, consequently, her brother's honor. What ensues is a story of revenge that ends with Anush scrambling mountains and valleys in folly until she ends her life by throwing herself down a cliff.

But that day he couldn't resist.

The distance between mother and son was shrinking more and more.

The ground melted Valodik's shoes. He walked up barefoot and stood in front of his mother. The fisher's wife had not seen Valodik; she had sensed him. The boy, struck dumb, had frozen and was looking at *fleeting* Zakyan Street.

Suddenly the wall of the library shook and the bundle of porn magazines in Valodik's hand fell and opened up in front of his mother's eyes. In shame, the red of the raspberries collected on his face and he fell to his knees. For a moment the mother and son's eyes were frozen and riveted on each other. At that same moment, Aralez's [35]head popped out of the corner, licked the woman's legs and the boy's face, and flew them a thousand kilometers away from Yerevan...

The *fleeting* city was visible to me in its entirety with a one-year interval...

I hate this restaurant. It's a crude construction decorated with eagles and stones on the outside. The snow of Ararat that had been planted on the roof was melting and rolling down like piss.

It was a banquet. The president's wife was standing by the door in a strait jacket ordering the orderly to let me in. It's repeating again?

"Are there many people?"

"No, just us. Napoleon just left. When did they let you out of Sevan?"

"A week ago... on Wednesday..."

35 Aralez is a town in Ararat Province in Armenia. It is also a mythical canine-looking creature known to lick the wounds of wounded soldiers.

"It's wonderful... Isn't there another Turk to save me from this asylum? I'm not a whore... Well, say it, say that nothing... nothing happened between us..."

I was looking puzzled to my left and right when I saw Nana. She was turning all the men's penises into stone with her Medusan gaze.

I had no desire to speak with her...

"Grig? You don't say hi anymore?"

"Hi..."

"I heard you got married..."

"I get the impression that the entire nation is thinking about getting me married."

"Why are you surprised? It's from you, no, that our future crown prince will be born?"

"A year ago it could've even been from you..."

"Congratulations," she cut me off and with that stopped my nose from bleeding.

"For what?"

"Did I receive a medal?"

I wanted to ask what medal when she handed over a package.

"And this is a gift for you..."

"There was no need." the Medusan Viagra started to take effect.

There was nothing about the box that made it stand out.

I crumpled the gold, crinkly paper and tore it open. Deer antlers rocked in my hands. The hall suddenly became dark and Gagik and I appeared on the wall that had turned into a screen.

"Slow down... Gag, are you doing it on purpose?"

"How's your dog?"

"There's no dog... I have a cat now..."

"Isn't a cat more dangerous? If you leave it hungry for a day, it'll jump and gouge your eyes out."

"Gag, I want to buy flowers for Nana..."

"Let's buy some..."

"Stop. Let me get out..."

With eyes as beautiful as the eyes of a foal, with disheveled hair, and inch-long eyelashes, Gagik's pop art face appeared on the screen.

The commercial ended with a photograph of the president holding Ararat. Nana finished her interview and shoved the microphone between her breasts.

"Where's that friend of yours?"

"Where should he be? He went back to Sevan with your son..."

"Why didn't you go?"

"Are you really that stupid?"

The minister screwed Nana on the spot, on her feet...

What could I do? I had no choice but to prance around with the antlers on my head. "System's" heavy metal boiled inside of me. They just missed catching me, or else I would've pulled Ararat off the brow of the restaurant and hit the asshole's head with it.

"I knew it, I knew that you were a bastard and that you would disgrace me like this in the end..."

Those present froze on the spot. I put my hand in my pocket, took out the condom I had stolen from Gagik, stuck it on my forehead and, not paying attention to Nana's bleating, I started to shoot, shoot, shoot at the minister...

The water was hot. It stung the scar on my back. I assaulted her.

"Grig, you'll kill me," Anna was constantly kissing my mouth...

"No one has died of it yet."

"When you say no one, who do you mean?"

Her body squished like marmalade. My sticky finger reminded me that the condom that Gagik had given me was with me. My heart sank for a moment.

"Do you love me," she asked.

"I do..."

"Don't lie," she said and, grabbing a clump of my hair in her fist, smashed my head against the wall.

"Are you nuts?"

"You don't love me. If you loved me you'd be with me without that."

I pressed her hips and penetrated. I heard a squeak. A gush of blood rolled down to my knee and left rusty marks on the white of the bathroom.

"I told you, didn't I, that you'd kill me?"

My phone roared. Tram sparks appeared in my eyes when I saw Gagik's number. He had sent a text message.

"I love you, love you, want you..."

I withdrew... The minister was standing in front of the theater's main entrance. Two meatheads were guarding his back.

"Who's that guy you're hanging out with?"

"Dad, I love Grig."

"That drug addict?"

"Yeah, that drug addict..."

"Bring me a broom!"

They brought the broom solemnly, upholding all the subtleties of a ritual. The minister took the broom and smacked Anna's face. Blood spurted out of her nose, turning her father's beard red.

"I'll kill you!" The girl cursed her father with her eyes closed like my cat. "Dad, when are you going to die?"

Anna's sobs gradually turned into a duet. She's holding onto my wrist and forcing me to sing the high notes. I'm screaming way and way out of tune. Suddenly I turn around and what do I see? The hall is filled to the brim. The audience is clapping, prompting the lyrics of the song, spitting, and throwing rotten eggs.

"Do you see that door? That artificial, decorative door? Open it and enter the stage." Anna's operatic voice scratched my rock-accustomed ears.

"But we're already on stage."

"The mise en scène is like that. Grig, hurry up..."

I ran, opened the door, and...

They are demolishing my house.

The steel ball was opening ball-sized passageways in the walls. The throat of the whale, choked by dust and stone, would not let me in. Mom? Mom!

My mother was sitting on packages under the window crying. Her eyes widened so much in confusion and pain that the windows shattered into pieces.

"See what it has come to?"

"Thank God..."

"Why are you thanking God?"

"Mom, you recognize me, no?"

"Do I recognize myself to recognize you?"

"You don't recognize me?"

"You're crazy... Stay away, stay away from me... They took the house from my hands and destroyed it..."

"Mom!"

"I told you a thousand times to go and register everything in your name... I told you, didn't I, that everything is possible in this country. They'll even steal and sell the life you lived. How can anyone call this a life? It's been ten years and we still haven't been able to cover your father with a stone..."

My nose bled and immediately I heard the voice of the bull.

Investigator Gasparyan fixed his eyes into mine, puffed out his cheeks, and roared:

"Do you really have documents like that?"

"Like what?"

"That you're a descendant of the royal dynasty of Cilicia..."

"I do..."

"I'm not saying good for you, even though my people were ordinary farmers. Instead, it seems our positions have reversed. I'm joking..."

"You really like joking, huh?"

"I was right to accuse you of attempting to kill the minister. I was right..."

The grandmother's ghost whirred in my head. The fire and snow were not late. My house--or what was left of it--the trees, and my cat's grave suffocated in the smoke and froze in the white.

One of the tongues of the flames pulled out a drawer from the dresser, took out the document that proves my royal heredity, lifted it higher and higher out of the house, and lapped it up.

Only the writing *"Ne dazhdyoshsya menya, petlya"* remained on the wall.

"Grigor, in our last conversation you said that you lived in a *fleeting* city. Many people did not understand your thought. Please explain."

"A year ago, I didn't know where the *fleeting* could take someone. Even though, in my mind, I was standing firmly on the ground, I was the *Fleeting* One. Now a huge, one-million strong city is *fleeting*. And it's going so fast that you can't keep up with it. In just a few days your way of thinking can change so much that you don't even recognize yourself anymore."

"That's interesting. In that case I will try to give more or less the same questions as I gave a year ago. Grigor, has there ever been someone for you that you considered an authority and wanted to resemble?"

"I don't remember. Generally speaking, the first thing human psychology tends to misrepresent is civilization. In any given realm of influence, people have a tendency to turn themselves into idols for their subjects..."

"Many of your ancestors were killed in the Genocide. If I'm not mistaken, you're one of the descendants of the royal dynasty of Cilicia, and should justice be served, it's possible that you'll be proclaimed the prince of Cilicia."

"This is the first time I'm hearing such nonsense..."

"Grigor, have there ever been moments when your imagination tried to suppress or silence your reason?"

"Sure... Even now, I have a feeling that my cat is still alive."

"And do you consider yourself a lucky person?"

"Yes, I'm the luckiest, because I have nothing to lose."

"Grigor, if I'm not mistaken, there's a strange text in your room. Did you write it?"

"How could I be the one to write such stupidity?"

"And what does it say?"

"Ne dazhdyoshsya menya, petlya."

into Heaven... It's good the rope didn't scrape you much..."

I wanted to say something good, but couldn't. Edita went into the cross window and...

A red sparrow flew up and split the borderline...

P.S.

Grigor and Gagik met one year later.

Gagik was going to university and Grig had just come out of the staparan.[36] They decided to go see the statue by Kazirok.[37] Then they went inside the cafe and also saw the statues of four writers there.

Gagik had cut his hair very short.

"Vahagn came a month ago," he said, stirring his coffee.

"Was it good?"

"Joyous..."

"Did you finish your cartoon?"

"No. I haven't thought about it since I left university. What are you doing?"

"Nothing... Any news from Edita?"

"No, why?"

Edita died in a plane crash one month after fleeing Yerevan. She probably didn't die. In any case, her body hadn't been found.

Before getting on the plane, she had sent a strange text message to Grig:

"Every time I go abroad and pass through security, I feel that I'll find myself in heaven..."

Gagik didn't stay long. His girlfriend was waiting for

---

36 A staparan is a place where roaming drunk or drugged people are taken to be sobered up. The process involves hosing down the person with cold water until he or she comes to. The person is usually released the following day.
37 Kazirok is a little cafe next to Martiros Saryan's statue.

him by Moscow Cinema. He didn't tell Grig that he had a girlfriend. He said he was hurrying to get to the opening of the festival. Grig asked for the bill, he tried to get up, but his legs wouldn't let him. He remembered the cat that played with the sun and he raised his right hand.

To Gagik it seemed like his friend was saying goodbye from a distance. He turned around and:

"We'll meet again?" he asked.

"Definitely..."

But summer reminded both of them that they live in a *FLEETED* city where there is nothing other than buildings. And both of them understood that they would never see each other again...

20.04 - 7.11.2007
Not counting July and August.